BEFORE 'THE AM
AN EVEN MORE
TOOK PLACE IN

The story of the Lutz family was told in the book and the movie 'The Amityville Horror.' They fled from their home on Ocean Avenue one night in terror, convinced the house was possessed by unspeakably evil forces.

The Lutzes escaped with their lives. The previous tenants of the house did not.

In November 1974, the DeFeo family was living in the house on Ocean Avenue. One night Ronald DeFeo, Jr, the eldest of the five DeFeo children, saw a hand draped in black reach out to him and heard a voice. The voice said, 'Kill.'

Ronald took a rifle and cold-bloodedly murdered the six members of his family.

Was Ronald DeFeo, Jr possessed?

Why were none of the victims awakened by the first shots?

Were the shots silenced by some unseen force?

FINALLY!
MURDER IN AMITYVILLE!
THE WHOLE HORRIFYING STORY!

Hans Holzer

Murder in Amityville

Futura

A Futura Book

First published in Great Britain by
Futura Publications Limited in 1980
Reprinted 1981, 1983 (twice), 1985

ISBN 0 7088 1819 6

Filmset, printed and bound in Great Britain by
Hazell Watson & Viney Limited,
Member of the BPCC Group,
Aylesbury, Bucks

Futura Publications
A Division of
Macdonald & Co (Publishers) Ltd
Maxwell House
74 Worship Street
London EC2A 2EN
A BPCC plc Company

Acknowledgments

Special thanks for their cooperation on this project are due to William E. Weber and Bernard Burton, attorneys; to John Nicnick and Andrew Wiesner, producer and director of the TV film 'Murder in Amityville'; to Armstrong Productions, Allentown, Pa.; to Muriel Balash, film editor; and to Resa Cronin Typing Services.

Contents

Foreword

In the middle of a cold, wet night in November 1974, 22-year-old Ronald DeFeo woke from a disturbed sleep, got out of bed like a zombie and took down his .35 caliber rifle. Then he went from room to room and methodically killed his entire family in cold blood.

Within minutes, his father and mother, his brothers, 11 and 9, and his two sisters, 13 and 18, lay dead in their own blood. Then Ronald calmly telephoned police and reported finding his family murdered on returning home from work.

Forty hours later, Ronald confessed he had done the killing. But he did not know how and why. Nor, frankly, did the police. Nevertheless, young DeFeo was convicted of second degree murder and sentenced to six consecutive terms of 25 years each – a total of 150 years in prison. He's been serving his life sentence ever since at Dannemora. Though he knows he did the shooting, he still does not know why.

Ever since the family had bought the old house on Amityville's Ocean Avenue, young Ronald had felt strange in it. Three times he ran away from home, and three times he was brought back. The last time he pleaded with his father, to let him go, he knew he was going to kill them all someday, but nobody would listen to the boy then.

Still, the father also knew something was not quite right about the three-story Dutch Colonial house built in 1928. Certain strange happenings occurred that caused him to call in a priest, to place holy statues of Catholic saints all over the house and even in the garden around it, and to plant tulips. All the plants died.

According to Sgt Pat Cammarato of the Amityville Police, tragedy had struck down every family that ever lived in that house. The Long Island newspaper asked, 'Was DeFeo possessed by a supernatural force that night he methodically slaughtered his entire family?'

Even the court-appointed defense attorney William Weber now thinks there is more to this case than what has so far come out. He may appeal the verdict on the grounds of 'unusual circumstances' beyond DeFeo's control.

This is not the first time a man with psychic inclinations was 'taken over' by residues of life forces long dormant in a place where great tragedies have occurred.

The story of *Sybil* has become a bestseller as was *The Three Faces of Eve* before her. A few weeks ago, a man named Arthur Bicknell won freedom after a psychiatrist proved that one of his multiple personalities had committed the crimes he was convicted for. But the DeFeo case is not just one of split personality: it involves *possession*.

WHAT EXACTLY IS POSSESSION?

'The man is possessed,' or 'Whatever possessed him?' are popular phrases describing a person who doesn't act quite like himself – that is to say, a person with marked personality changes so obvious that everyone can see them. 'Possessed by the furies' is a more poetic way of expressing the thought that a person is being led by some form of madness.

Take Jane X. She's an ordinary housewife. She lives with her husband and three children in a suburb of one of America's largest cities. She is thirty years old, has never had the slightest interest in occult matters, goes to church whenever she can't escape going, reads very little, and then only reads subjects of average nature. One day Jane starts behaving like a totally different person. She has new ideas, knowledge of places or situations she couldn't possibly have seen, and even her facial expressions are no longer her own. Gradually she speaks with someone else's tongue. Not only does she say things that she couldn't possibly say when she was just plain Jane, but she reacts differently to the world around her. Her behavior becomes so unusual that a physician is called in. After carefully investigating the circumstances, he will probably recommend that a psychiatrist be called into the case. The psychiatrist will question the new Jane. After a while he will come to the conclusion that Jane has suffered a nervous breakdown or perhaps, even worse, exhibits signs of schizophrenia or split personality. He may recommend treatment in an institution, or he may suggest private analysis, depending upon the situation.

Jack S. is a well-to-do sales manager for an Eastern company. He's been married for twenty-two years, has a happy home life, nice hobbies, and really no problems. One day he enters a local restaurant, takes out a gun and shoots four people he has never met before. Afterwards, he remembers absolutely nothing. He is routinely sentenced to a long jail term, and branded a wanton murderer. To the criminologist, to the physician, to the judge, this is merely a case of sudden insanity – criminal insanity perhaps, but without any unusual overtones. Some of these cases certainly are. Some are not. What I have just mentioned are two classic cases of *possession*. They are not actual cases, and the names mentioned are fictitious, but I can match these hypothetical cases over and over with real stories from my files. The purpose of crystallizing here two of the most serious forms possession can take is to bring out how easy it is to fall prey to misconceptions regarding possession. Possession can be masked in many ways. This does not mean that one should become hysterical and look for real possession in every case of personality change or whenever someone acts strangely. Nothing would be further from the purpose of this report. I do not wish to alarm anyone or to start an entire movement of "possession hunters" in the fashion of the medieval witch hunters. Generally speaking, actual cases are rarely as defined and as clear-cut as the two examples I have just quoted. I will go into the specifics of each case when necessary, but suffice it to say that possession follows no simple law. That is to say, it may follow many laws of which we are only dimly aware. It can come suddenly or gradually. It can come partially or totally. It can even disappear at times without anyone doing anything about it, although *that* is decidedly rare.

The word possession comes from the Latin *possedere*, which means, quite obviously, 'to possess, to own, to take over.' Taking the word's two components, however, we find possession consisting of post and sedere. The latter word means 'to sit, to be situated,' and the 'post' generally stands for 'after' or 'beyond.' Thus, when we translate freely, possedere means 'to sit on top of.' It is interesting to note in this connection that in the Middle Ages, a popular conception of possession included a wraith or gnome sitting on top of the possessed individual, pushing down upon his or her body, causing nightmares and other forms of altered states of consciousness. The concept of the word *possession* indicates that it relates to a total takeover, and total control of an individual by another individual or some outside force. Possession excludes the will of the possessed. It presupposes the inability of the victim to overcome the attacking force and in submitting to it, becomes its tool.

What exactly is possession in terms of various approaches? We can distinguish between the medical, religious, popular, and, finally, parapsychological approach to the problem of possession. In a *medical* sense, the verdict is likely to be schizophrenia or some other form of mental or even physical derangement. The medical profession on the whole does not acknowledge the existence of separate entities apart from the flesh-and-blood personality of the victim. In fact, medical experts barely recognize the possibility that man has something more than a physical body. Medicine has as yet not come to terms with the entire problem of human personality-soul-spirit. In medical terms then, the possibility of one person being possessed by another against his will is entirely inconceivable, with the sole marginal exception of hypnosis, of course, or some other form of undue but direct influence. When a person shows marked personality changes and acts in a way contrary to his or her previous habits, the medical doctor will look for personality defects rather than the presence of a new or outside personality. With the advent of psychiatry, the reality of secondary and even tertiary personalities within the personality of one human being has become an accepted fact. But these secondary and tertiary personalities are still considered parts of the original personality, and in the view of most medical men, such parts must be reunited with the main personality or entirely destroyed if the patient is to become well again. A celebrated case in point was the case later dramatized in *The Three Faces of Eve*, in which such split-off parts of personality were dealt with in great detail. The medical doctors dealing with the case at the time came to the conclusion that the second and third personalities displayed by Eve were in fact only underlying split-off parts of Eve's own self in the end.

I have, on careful study of this and similar cases, come to the conclusion that this is not necessarily the answer, but that there may be another parapsychological explanation for the strange personality splits within one individual as shown in the case of *The Three Faces of Eve*. The possibility of interference from a dimension other than the physical one must not be discounted. This holds particularly true in instances where the individual displays amazing skills and abilities incompatible with his or her upbringing, training, and general background. Some medical men and especially psychiatrists like to explain this as latent abilities which are awakened by the process of splitting-off secondary personalities. But this does not seem to be a satisfactory explanation, since many such talents could not possibly have been dormant in the individuals concerned and could not have been acquired by osmosis or in some marginal fashion. For instance, the ability to speak a foreign language with great fluency or the ability to drive a car when the individual has had no training whatsoever in either of these areas – this cannot simply be explained by dormant talents present all the time within the individual. Such skill must enter the conscious or unconscious of the person somewhere along the line, and this has not been the case in a number of instances known to me. The only logical explanation for such behavior seems to be the transference of knowledge or skills from the outside; that is to say, by an outside entity functioning in another dimension. To put it into the vernacular, I am convinced that in certain cases of this type, in which secondary and other multiple personalities have occurred, there exists a situation wherein a living individual with full consciousness, but functioning in a nonphysical dimension, operates the body and mind of a living person. This relationship between a deceased mind and a living mind may be contrary to orthodox medical view, but the evidence points strongly in the direction that such a relationship does, in fact, exist.

Possession in terms of the *religious* establishment is nothing but the entrance of an outside force, generally evil, into the soul of the concerned individual. Whether or not the term demonic possession is used, the inference is that a living entity has entered the body of the victim in order to express its own will and frustrations. To the church, this is always evil and must be dealt with through exorcists. Not every religious community accepts this version, but the so-called orthodox faiths do believe in the existence of possession and the need for exorcism. To this day, the Catholic Church retains the rite of exorcism in its scriptures. In an offshoot of orthodox Judaism called the Chasidic cult, belief in the *dybbuk*, or possessing spirit, is still extant and is dealt with similarly as in the Roman Catholic exorcism. In both cases, the possessing spirit is asked to leave and if it refuses, it is forced out of the body of the victim by various means. In bygone days these means included everything from torture to bizarre threats and incantations believed to be effective by the sheer power of the arrangement of phrases. When only words were used to drive out the evil spirits the matter had either no effect or, through a form of hypnotic suggestion, resulted in freeing the victim from its possessor. However, when physical torture was used (in theory to destroy the possessing entity, but in practice only hurting the victim) the results were not as fortunate. The church believed that the death of a possessed individual in the process of trying to free that person from its possessor was unavoidable if the evil spirit was stronger than the victim. The church felt that it was better to destroy both than permit the victim to exist under the spell of its possessor and possibly harm others. The number of unfortunate people who were thus tortured to death by seemingly well-meaning exorcists of religious background is considerable.

In terms of modern psychology, this is what happened. The priest or minister held himself up as the representative of the forces of God and of good faced with the presence of what he considered an evil spirit in the hapless body of the victim. He entirely overlooked the victim's own involvement in the matter and considered it strictly an affair between himself and the devil, represented by the evil spirit possessing the victim in front of him. With every blow struck against the possessing entity, the exorcist's religious fanaticism rose to new heights, and if the body of the possessed expired in the process, well, at least the soul was now free to go up to heaven and worry no more about being possessed. The exorcist could rightly claim victory over another demon. The church had once again proven its superiority over the forces of darkness. This was psychologically satisfactory to the exorcist in that it reconfirmed his divine mission in driving out demons at all costs. But we must never forget that the true fanatic is lacking in self-respect and personal emotional security. He seeks his fulfillment in the imposition of his views or ideology upon others. Rather than seeking individual acclaim, he prefers being an instrument for some large force for good or other ideological concept; in this force, he is merely one small part or tool. Thus he obtains personal emotional security from the knowledge, true or false, that there are many others who agree with him and support his actions. If the exorcist succeeded, it had to be proven by the victim's rational behavior, but in terms of religious exorcism, it was also proven by the victim's further relationship with the church and God. If the victim showed any changes from his or her previous attitude in this respect, or if the victim deviated even in the slightest from the official line, the exorcism could not be called successful.

If the victim survived religious exorcism, with its possessor intact, then clearly the exorcist had but two choices: destroy the victim altogether and thus take care of both the victim and possessor, or to place the victim into permanent confinement where he could do no harm to others. At the same time, the victim became available to the 'forces of mercy,' should these forces decide to rescue the victim, after all, without benefit of the exorcist.

Thus, countless wretches, whose sole problem had been possession, were thrust into dungeons under the supervision of the Inquisition or the church in general, and expired eventually through neglect.

The *popular* attitude towards possession combines certain elements of the religious and medical approaches, but adds another dimension – that of fear and superstition. Both physicians and churchmen knew very well that touching the body of a possessed individual could have no dire consequences for them, since the body belonged to the victim and not to the possessor. But in the popular view, the very touch of the possessed was poisonous and had to be avoided at all costs. Being in the presence of a possessed person and looked at by such an individual could also have terrible consequences. In the southern part of Europe, this popular superstition became confused with the evil eye concept, and people thought that the casting of glances by a possessed person upon a healthy one was in itself sufficient grounds for a healthy person to fall ill and perhaps become possessed himself. In antiquity, it was customary to drive a possessed person out of town, with the idea that as long as the individual was no longer in the immediate vicinity, one couldn't care less where else the possessed one might cause damage. Driving the possessed from the confines of one's village eventually led to chasing the victim out, and stoning the individual at the same time, in the hope that a lucky stone might finish the person off altogether. In that case, the stone that made the perfect hit was not thrown by the individual actually throwing it, but directed by some *superior force* from above and thus entirely acceptable as an act of fate. Whenever a person who had the earmarks of the possessed entered the community, he had to be avoided at all costs. 'Possessed by the furies' was the term used for such individuals who were thought to be the victims of evil spirits because of some evil deed they themselves had done.

That evil invites evil is a concept still prevalent among many primitive people and even among many not-so-primitive ones. Anything a possessed person touched had to be destroyed immediately. In extreme cases, if the possessed touched another human being, the village would destroy that human being, or at least ostracize him, lest the entire community be affected. In some respects, therefore, possession was considered by society as a communicable problem, a disease, something one could catch from the victim if one wasn't careful. Under no circumstances could or should one undertake anything to fight against possession. To help the possessed individual was out of the question. The results could only be negative and involve innocents in the process of possession.

Fear, along with total misconception regarding what possession was, helped create a false image in the popular mind. Ever since the established church had made it into the work of the devil during the twelfth and thirteenth centuries, the popular version of what happened to the victim included some form of diabolical influence. Whether it was a demon or underling of the devil, or the Great One himself, inevitably there was at work some hellish play that created the dismal state of possession in the victim. It never occurred to the popular mind that possession could also be the result of benevolent interference or anything less than devilish machinations. Anyone acting under the influence of another individual had to be possessed by the devil and his minions. To the church, of course, such popular attitudes were pleasing, since they helped reinforce its hold, which had been carefully nurtured over the centuries by threats of fear, upon the people. Threats that sprang from the official dogmatic line promised dire consequences for one's soul, and fear of contact with those clearly not in God's grace would have similar results for oneself.

Only with the advent of *parapsychology* as a serious scientific form of inquiry has possession as a phenomenon of the human personality been brought into an objective focus devoid of all religious prejudices and medical condemnation. The phenomenon emerges as an intensely human, but at the same time paranormal, experience possible only through the interrelationship of two entities. These two entities may be both of the physical world or, as in the majority of cases, in the physical and the nonphysical world.

But in each and every case of true possession we are dealing with *two separate individuals* no matter how restricted or structured in their individual consciousness.

Originally parapsychology also tended to consider the phenomena involving possession as part of the as yet unchartered depths of human personality. Indeed, to this very day, there are some parapsychologists who cannot get themselves to accept the reality of nonphysical entities existing in another dimension than earth. These parapsychologists prefer to force the phenomena of possession into the narrow channels of one-entity concepts. To them, possession involves only abnormal activities of the personality itself. To be sure, they are not suggesting, as psychiatrists are likely to, that possession involves abnormalities of the mind in terms of mental illness. What these parapsychologists suggest, however, as a possible explanation of possession, is a kind of extension of human personality beyond the boundaries presently known. Under this extension, the human personality becomes aware of knowledge, abilities, and other evidential material from beyond its own confines. Such an explanation of possession is, to my mind, a tortured one, and it does not cover some of the incidents involved in some possession cases which cannot be explained on such a basis. These cases clearly involve a completely alien personality which is frequently in total conflict with the rest of the personality, as evidenced by the personality's behavior, both normal and under possession. Again, to put it into the vernacular, to such parapsychologists the victim manufactures the possession entity out of his or her own unconscious, for various reasons. These reasons may involve the desire to manifest greater popularity or interest and register more strongly with the environment, or they may stem from emotional problems and indicate merely the individual's desire to express a greater variety of traits than the individual does in the full conscious state. With this explanation, a possessing entity again becomes a subordinate part of the personality, similar to the conventional explanation so frequently offered by orthodox psychiatrists. The only difference here is that the psychiatrist regards such splitting of personality essentially a malignant process, whereas the parapsychologist considers this a positive factor, indicating greater personality potentials in the individual concerned, and not necessarily a form of mental illness.

In psychic research the method employed presupposes the existence of a separate entity causing possession to take place. This entity is a human being generally no longer in the living body. Occasionally there are reports of *possession by a living person* of another. This, however, is a combination of telepathy, sometimes involves hypnosis, and always calls for an interrelationship between possessed and possessor.

The overwhelming majority of cases, however, involve possession of a living person by the spirit of a *dead* individual. For a variety of reasons the dead individual wishes to use the physical, emotional, and mental faculties of the living being for his own ends, regardless of consequences and regardless of the wishes of the instrument used. However, I have found that it is quite impossible for possession to take place, if the individual who is possessed does not open the gates in some fashion to the possessor. Generally, this is not done consciously, but it may be the result of unconscious desire or weakness which allow possession to take place.

Evil remains evil, whether in the body or out of it. Since individuals differ widely in their appetites and moral standards, and since people take their individuality with them to the other side of life, it stands to reason that among the multitudes of discarnates populating the limitless realms of the nonphysical world, there are many who cannot adjust to that world and to its standards. They long for the physical world and the appetites associated with it, and they will do everything in their power to return if only through the precarious hold they may exercise upon a living person on the earth plane. This is not a matter of vicarious thrills experienced through the sensory apparatus of another in possession. They *are* the other person and experience these sensations *directly* and *intimately*.

In possession, the possessing personality enters the physical body of the victim through one of the solar plexuses, that is, the psychic 'opening gates' located at the top of the head and in the stomach region. As the possessor gains hold of nerve ganglia at these points, the entity then connects with the nervous system of the individual and merges in its own personality fields with the electromagnetic personality field of the host personality. If the merger is complete, the host's personality may be entirely displaced by the possessor's own personality. In the majority of possessions, this merger is less than complete. As a result, there are fluctuations in the impact of the possessing entity. At times the merger is complete, and the possessor speaks as himself. At other times, the host personality is again in control and returns to his or her normal self.

The reasons for possession may vary greatly according to the individual character of the possessing spirits. They may be merely delusions to continue a physical type of life through another individual, or it may be due to recognition that some particular individual is especially suited to continue the needs and unfinished business of the deceased individual. In some cases the living person appeals to the power instinct of the discarnate. Often, the possessor fancies himself or herself in the notion of playing Svengali to some meek Trilby on the earth plane, enjoying the power play as an antidote to the boredom encountered on the spiritual level. This occurs because the discarnate has not yet understood the attractions and possibilities at that level and continues to regard everything from the physical point of view alone.

Willingness to be possessed is by no means as far-fetched as it may sound. To a large number of people, the idea of having a superior will superimposed on their own will is not only acceptable but desirable. It eliminates the need to make decisions, shifts the burden of failure from the self to the person of another, and, in general, creates a kind of dependency, which to some is a comfortable refuge from the pressures of the environment. Passive willingness to accept dominance by another is *always* present in cases of possession. In the majority of situations the victim is not even aware of it, but it is nevertheless part of the syndrome. At the very least, fear of the superior influence of the possession entity, and conviction that nothing can be done about it, are present in all such cases.

1

The Facts of November 13, 1974

If it weren't for a sensational best seller and a subsequent motion picture, the town of Amityville, Long Island would hardly evoke any great interest on the part of the public. As it is, Amityville has become identified with what is being sold as an outstanding horror story and which may, in the final analysis, only be a well-publicized, run-of-the-mill haunted house story with overtones of mass murder. Be this as it may, Amityville, Long Island will never forget the night of November 13, 1974, because it was during that night, or rather in the early morning hours, 3:15 A.M. to be precise, that a crime took place which had such dire consequences not only for its victims, of course, or for the perpetrator of the crime, but for the entire population of Amityville. Because of this crime, and what it brought in its wake, Amityville will never be the same. The people, at first stunned by the severity of the crime, later intrigued by overtones of the supernatural, finally were convinced that they had become the victims of a curse. Promotional activities on the behalf of a bestseller purported to be 'a true story,' which the townspeople say it isn't, and a motion picture which attracted even more of the idle curious and of the not so idle curious to the little town on Long Island, which prefers to be left to its own pace and peace.

Nevertheless, Amityville, Long Island will be a name long remembered as the site of a notorious crime, and perhaps in the years to come may even pass into the dictionary as a description of horror.

But even today, five years after the crime, Amityville

is far from a horrible place. It is a small town without particular distinction, about an hour's ride from New York City, not too far from the ocean, but far enough to require people to get into their cars if they want to enjoy the beach. Many of the houses in Amityville are expensive, many are not; the main street seems quiet, and very little in Amityville would attract attention had it not been for what transpired there in 1974.

It was on the morning of November 14, 1974, that local police were called to the house at 112 Ocean Avenue, owned by Ronald DeFeo, an automobile dealer. The call was for a grim reason; Ronald DeFeo, Jr., then 22 years old, reported finding six members of his family murdered in their beds. When police arrived at the Dutch Colonial house, they found that young DeFeo had indeed spoken the truth. Shot at close range by a .35 caliber rifle, the six members of DeFeo's family lay dead in their beds in both the downstairs and the upstairs portion of the house. The police found the bodies of Donald DeFeo, Sr.; his wife Louise; daughters Dawn, 18, and Allison, 13; and sons Mark, 12, and John Matthew, 7. Ronald, Jr. told police that he had discovered the bodies when he returned from work. But forty hours later Ronald DeFeo, Jr. was charged with the murder of his family, and placed into custody. The murder weapon, a rifle, was later recovered from a creek near Amityville where DeFeo had tossed it.

In the early stages of the story, when DeFeo had just been taken into custody, seemingly conflicting accounts were published by the press or mentioned on television. According to Channel 5, New York, police revealed that Ronald DeFeo, Jr. had been under special narcotics probation at the time he committed the crime, they made a point of recalling young DeFeo's conviction for stealing a $1750 outboard motor in September of 1974 and even suggested that DeFeo might have stolen $19,000 in cash and checks from his grandfather's automobile dealership in Brooklyn, where he used to work. They even charged a fellow employee named Arthur Belin, with aiding and abetting him in the crime, but none of this stood up later and rapidly disappeared from the discussion of DeFeo's reasons for having committed the crime.

Other points made during the early stages of the investigation later proved to be groundless. According to Channel 5, New York, Ronald DeFeo, Jr. allegedly told police that he had administered heavy doses of barbiturates to his family on the night they were killed, by adding the drugs to the family dinner. But this turned out to be not true.

Meanwhile, on November 18, 1974, a funeral was held for the six murdered members of the DeFeo family and a local attorney by the name of Richard H. Wyssling presented himself as DeFeo's attorney.

But during a pre-trial hearing young DeFeo testified that the police had beaten a confession out of him, and that he now felt his earlier admission of having committed the crime was no longer valid. DeFeo was lodged in the Suffolk County Jail at Riverhead, and the long arduous path of the trial took its course. In the summer of 1975, William E. Weber was appointed by the court to defend DeFeo. At first DeFeo was anything but cooperative, refusing to discuss the crime itself, but readily talking about his own life. Gradually, however, Weber managed to gain DeFeo's confidence and in his own mind get a better perspective of what might have happened that night. Ronald DeFeo, Jr. was well treated by his family, to the extent that he never lacked in any essentials and often had more money than he might have needed. Somehow he got hooked on heroin during his teenage years, and underwent psychiatric therapy on several occasions. However, there is nothing to indicate that he was actually on drugs at the time of the murder or in the period preceeding it.

Ronald DeFeo, Sr. was general manager of his father-in-law's Buick dealership in Brooklyn. Young DeFeo freely admitted to me that he and his father did not always see eye to eye, and that tension between them erupted into arguments at various times over the years. Ronald's mother Louise, on the other hand, had a close relationship to her son and there was no tension between her and Ronald, nor were there any problems between Ronald and his brothers and sisters. On the whole, the DeFeo family was no better or worse than other families of their social and economic background and when they moved from their Brooklyn apartment to the much larger Amityville house, they were at first somewhat overawed by the comparative luxury of their new surroundings, but quickly took to the environment and became part of the local scene.

From the District Attorney's point of view, this was a classic murder case. The bodies were all too much in evidence; the motive, a considerable amount of money and jewelry which the elder DeFeo had allegedly placed into a box hidden away under a floor board of one of the closets. These were not found, however, and the accused stated that his father had cleaned out the secret cache several days before the crime. When William Weber took over the defense of Ronald DeFeo, he was faced with an existing confession, obtained prior to his involvement in the case. Ronald DeFeo never denied the shooting, although he was equally frank in stating that he didn't remember it. He is quoted stating to his defense attorney, 'I must have done it because I don't know who else could have done it, but believe me if I had a choice, I wouldn't have done it.' DeFeo continued to withhold details of the actual deed, but he freely admitted to Weber that he had vomited immediately afterwards, had cleaned up, and finally decided to take the gun and place it where it would not easily be discovered. Defense attorney Weber put an experienced investigator, Herman Race, on the case. It was Race who discovered that Dawn, the 18 year old daughter, had unburned gunpowder particles on her nightgown. To Race, a retired New York City detective working on the homicide squad, this meant that she must have also fired a gun that fateful night. Immediately upon discovering this peculiar bit of evidence, Weber confronted his client. Why hadn't Ronald told Weber the entire truth? Ronald shook his head. Nobody would believe him, he replied. Weber pinpointed the direction he was heading. What about Ronald and his sister Dawn? Ronald admitted that he and Dawn had committed the crime together. According to him, and according to what he then told Weber, he had shot his parents although he failed to explain his reasons for it. Then, again, according to Ronald's earlier testimony, his sister Dawn took the rifle and shot the three other children. At that point, she allegedly went gunning for Ronald and he had to hide in the closet while she searched for him throughout the house. When she could not find him, she went back to sleep and it was then, according to Ronald, that he came out of the closet, took the gun and killed her, too. Much later, when I confronted him at Dannamora prison, he shook his head rather sadly, denying the whole thing. He assured me that he had done it all by himself; every one of the murders. It was at that time, when Weber first entered the case, that DeFeo claimed he had heard voices telling him what he had done. He himself did not recall any of it. He freely admitted that there had been a relationship between himself and his sister Dawn, despite their being brother and sister. None of this bothered him in the least. He did not share his parent's religious views, in fact he told me that when a priest was invited to the house by his late father, he left immediately because he did not want to be under the same roof with the priest.

When Weber heard about the alleged voices getting

DeFeo to kill he dismissed this as a sign of insanity, either temporary or permanent, perhaps induced by prior drug use.

Since there was no other reasonable explanation for the crimes, the defense strategy was to claim insanity for Ronald DeFeo, Jr. First, however, Weber tried unsuccessfully to suppress the confession obtained by the police in the first hours after the arrest, and when this was not possible, he stayed with the insanity defense. On November 21, 1975, the jury found DeFeo guilty of six counts of second degree murder and on December 4 of the same year he was sentenced to six consecutive terms of 25 years to life in prison. The court ruled that young DeFeo should serve his terms at Dannamora, a maximum security prison in upper New York State, close to the Canadian border. The town of Dannamora is the kind of place one would feel depressed in even if it didn't have the Clinton facility, as it is officially called. At this writing, Ronald DeFeo, who is now 26 years old and is reported to be a model prisoner, is at Dannamora prison, wondering what fate has in store for him for the rest of his life. To the court, to the jury, to the attorney who defended him, the case is closed. Except perhaps for new evidence that might somehow be uncovered. Attorney William Weber has an open mind about such unusual possibilities as possession, but until hard evidence can be presented sufficient to reopen the case, there is little he can or will do.

It is ironical that during the long trial and the many hearings the entire area of the supernormal was not even touched upon, yet after the house was sold to Mr and Mrs George Lutz, and reports of paranormal occurrences began to appear in the press, this entirely new aspect became evident. Unfortunately, none of this had been mentioned during the trial. Had it been, perhaps it would have been followed up by competent investigators unbiased by personal prejudices.

2

Hearing Before Trial: The Official Record

In the following pages I will attempt to give the most important passages from the actual trial records, as taken down by court stenographers and official recording clerks. I have eliminated duplication or questions of no relevance to what I consider the heart of this case: the question of supernormal influences upon young DeFeo at the time of the crime. But many of the questions and answers cast a revealing light upon DeFeo's character, and on the years before the crime was committed. They also show how the police apparatus and the courts cannot help but run in well-defined channels, following narrow tracks to their desired destination. There is little room in these proceedings for extraordinary aspects, no room at all for such matters as possession or influence of an entity from the past. Had such subjects been brought out, they would not have influenced the court, I think, unless they had been presented as a complete picture of the location itself where the crime was committed rather than as part of Ronald DeFeo's personal experiences. For it is Ronald's established psychic inclination, together with the background of the location of 112 Ocean Avenue, which furnished me with the leads toward the possibility of possession. Only if both of these elements are taken together and the location is investigated from as far back as one can reach, does a reasonable picture emerge. Nobody questions the fact that Ronald DeFeo killed six people at 112 Ocean Avenue; but could it be that he was the seventh victim, an instrument of evil from beyond what we conventionally call death, rather than a fully rational person, cunningly and cold-bloodedly planning the extermination of his family?

As the trial records will show, Ronald DeFeo, Jr changed his story many times, but in order to understand his reasons one must consider the circumstances under which he was interrogated. One must also consider the possibility of alien influences being present even then, causing him not always to act rationally. This is not meant to exonerate the young man of the horrid crime he committed, but merely an attempt to explore the underlying causes.

* * *

**SUPREME COURT OF THE STATE
OF NEW YORK
COUNTY OF SUFFOLK**

**THE PEOPLE OF THE STATE
OF NEW YORK** :
—against— : Indictment No. 1251-74

RONALD JOSEPH DE FEO, JR, :
Defendant. :

Riverhead, New York
September 22, 1975

BEFORE:

HON. THOMAS M. STARK, Justice

APPEARANCES:

HON. HENRY R. O'BRIEN, District Attorney of the County of Suffolk, by GERARD B. SULLIVAN, Assistant District Attorney, of Counsel, for the People

WILLIAM WEBER, ESQ., for the Defendant

(Court convened at 10:05 a.m.)

THE CLERK: Suppression hearing, People vs. Ronald Joseph DeFeo, Jr.

MR SULLIVAN: People are ready, sir.

THE COURT: Defendant ready?

MR WEBER: Defendant ready, your Honor.

THE COURT: Mr Weber, does your client still intent to rely on the defense of mental disease or defect? There was a notice served in the case back on May 15 pursuant to 250.10 of the Criminal Procedure Law.

MR WEBER: That is correct, your Honor.

THE COURT: As far as the trial of the indictment, he does definitely intend to rely on the defense of mental disease or defect?

MR WEBER: With the reservation that we may change the defense.

THE COURT: All right, my next question is this: Does your client still intend to raise the affirmative defense that he acted under extreme emotional disturbance pursuant to 125.25 of the Penal Law?

MR WEBER: At this point the answer is yes.

THE COURT: Does your client seek to suppress his written statement dated November 13, 1974?

MR WEBER: We seek to suppress every statement the defendant is alleged to have made while in custody.

THE COURT: He does intend to seek suppression of his written statement as well as any oral statements; is that correct?

MR WEBER: That is correct.

THE COURT: Now, he did not specify, as required by law, back in his original motion, what his grounds were. He merely claimed at that time that any statements were obtained by unlawful methods or means. In your subsequent motion you advance further grounds in support of the motion. You stated in your affidavit that he was held in custody for over 36 hours; that he was intentionally deprived of his rights to counsel; that he was severely beaten during his confinement and denied due process of law.

MR WEBER: I'd like to amend the severely beaten to include mental duress also, your Honor.

THE COURT: All right, I assume, of course, that, even though it doesn't appear clear from the papers, that the People have denied these allegations of fact?

MR SULLIVAN: That's true, Judge.

THE COURT: What is the extent of the People's proof?

MR SULLIVAN: We expect to call a series of police officers, Judge.

THE COURT: Now, to what extent is going to be the defendant's proof on the hearing?

MR WEBER: Well, your Honor, we have at least two attorneys, possibly three attorneys who will be testifying. We have at least three civilian witnesses, possibly five who will be called. I haven't heard anything about the district attorney producing any witnesses concerning the Massiah situation. The denial of the defendant of his right to counsel. That issue has been raised.

THE COURT: All right. Are you ready to proceed, Mr Sullivan?

MR SULLIVAN: The People are ready, your Honor.

THE COURT: Call your first witness on the hearing.

MR SULLIVAN: People call Detective Gaspar Randazzo.

DET. GASPAR RANDAZZO, Shield 410, First Squad Detectives, Suffolk County Police Department called as a witness in behalf of the People, having been first duly sworn, testified as follows:

Q: How long have you been a detective working with the First Squad?

A: Eight years.

Q: Does it cover the Amityville vicinity?

A: Yes it does.

Q: Now, I ask you if on the 13th day of November, 1974, you were working a tour of duty on that day?

A: Yes I was.

Q: Sometime during the course of your tour did you

receive a specific call to respond to some place in Amityville?

A: I did, sir.

The Court: What's the address to where you responded, officer, and what time?

The Witness: 112 Ocean Avenue. In Amityville Village.

The Court: What hour?

The Witness: At seven – approximately 1855 hours, which is 6:55.

Q: When you arrived there, what did you do? What did you see?

A: I was taken upstairs by an Amityville patrolman, and he showed me six people in bed. They were dead.

Q: Now, did you meet or speak with anybody else in that house at about that time?

A: Yes, Mr DeFeo. Ronald DeFeo.

Q: Do you see that person in this room now?

A: Yes, he is.

Q: Now, where was he when you first saw him on that day?

A: When I first saw him he was outside of the house.

Q: Did you have any words with him at that time?

A: Yes. I asked him to come inside into the kitchen.

Q: And when you arrived in the kitchen, what happened then?

A: I asked him what had happened, and he told me.

Q: And at that time that you had this initial conversation with him, what was his apparent emotional state?

A: He was crying and hysterical and visibly shaken up.

Q: Was there anybody else in the vicinity of the kitchen when you had this conversation with him?

A: Yes, there was a Detective Burkhardt and my – Detective Sergeant Jensen.

Q: Had other police officers involved in this investigation arrived at that time?

A: Yes, they started to arrive at that time, also. This is when I posted Police Officer Greguski at the front door not to let anybody else in.

Q: I want you to tell me further what was said in this conversation that you had with Mr DeFeo.

A: He went to work, and upon coming home he found the door locked. And he figured that there might have been something wrong because the doors were locked and he saw the cars outside the house. He went back . . . he was at a bar, and he spoke to somebody at the bar that he had . . . that he thinks that there is something wrong. And he came back to his home with someone else. I believe it was two other persons. And then he forced open the kitchen window, entered it; and when he went upstairs, he saw his whole family dead. Well, at that point, a priest came into the room, and he asked permission to speak to Mr DeFeo, which I said of course. And he spoke to Ronnie for a length of time.

Q: And thereafter did you have some further conversation with Ronald DeFeo?

A: I was asking him a few more questions as to how he got into the house. He said he forced his way in, and then at that point the homicide detectives arrived.

Q: All right. What, if anything, had you started to do as of the time the homicide detectives arrived?

A: I started to take a written statement, a scratch paper statement.

Q: Up to that point in time had any other members of the DeFeo family arrived there?

A: Yes. A Mr Rocco DeFeo and a Mr Brigante. Mr Brigante was Ronnie DeFeo's grandfather – Mrs DeFeo's father. And Mr DeFeo, naturally, was the deceased's father.

Q: What, if anything, occurred when Rocco DeFeo arrived?

A: Well, they wanted to go into the house. And in fact, they insisted on going into the house. I said they could not go into the house due to the fact that it was a crime scene, and I requested everybody to leave at that point.

Q: All right. Now I take you back to any further conversation that you had with Ronald DeFeo before the homicide detectives arrived.

A: Yes. I asked Mr DeFeo if he knew who could have possibly done this to his family. He was kind of reluctant to mention this, but he mentioned a man named Mr M., that he had a fight with the family, and he said that he could have possibly done this.

Q: Now, to the best of your recollection what time did detectives from the Homicide Squad of the Suffolk County Police Department arrive there?

A: This was at 7:15. Detectives Gozaloff, Napolitano, Shirvell, Grieco, Harrison, Reichert, and Detective Sergeant Barylski, all of the Homicide Squad. We obtained permission to use the house next door, which was the persons by the name of Ireland. At that point we moved everything to that position and set up a command post. At that point Detective Gozaloff started to interview Mr Ronald DeFeo.

CROSS-EXAMINATION BY MR WEBER:

Q: As you approached the building did you see any people standing outside of the front door?

A: Yes, I did.

Q: Did you see Ronnie DeFeo at that point?

A: Yes, he was outside the front door.

Q: Was he with anyone?

A: He was with two men, I believe, that were from the bar. There was Kelske and Yeswoit. Those were the two gentlemen I saw.

Q: Will you tell us again what you observed with Ronnie DeFeo the first time you began talking to him?

A: Well, he was crying. He was hysterical, visibly upset.

Q: Would you say that he was incoherent?

A: No. I spoke to him and he spoke to me.

Q: Was he hysterical?

A: He was crying. He was crying loudly and sobbing.

Q: Was Ronnie DeFeo crying while the priest was talking to him?

A: Yes, he was.

Q: Was he crying while you were talking to him?

A: Yes, he was.

Q: Thereafter he was not calm or cool, to use the vernacular, during your questioning?

A: No he was not.

Q: Was he basically the same way during the questioning, physically speaking, as when you had first observed him?

A: That's correct, sir.

Q: He was still in the hysterical mood?

A: He was still crying and sobbing and visibly upset.

Q: What time, officer, did you leave the DeFeo residence and move to the command post you set up in the Ireland house?

A: I think it was about 7:15. That's when Detective Sergeant Barylski came, and the Homicide Squad arrived, and they took over the investigation at that point.

Q: Did you see any member of Ronnie DeFeo's family talking with him up to the point where you began taking him to the Ireland house?

A: No.

Q: Was he in any protective custody at that point?

A: No, sir.

Q: Was he in any custody at all.

A: No, sir.

Q: At the point that you began taking him to the

Ireland house, was he in any way suspected as having been involved in this crime?

A: No, sir.

Q: So everything that occurred up to that point was purely investigatory; is that correct?

A: That's correct, sir.

Q: Officer, at about eleven or 11:30 were you approached by an attorney at the premises?

A: I was approached by a man who said that he was a friend of the family, and he had said that he was an attorney.

THE COURT: Did you make a note of who this man was?

THE WITNESS: No, sir, I did not.

Q: After you had a conversation with this individual, officer, what did you do or what did you say to him?

A: He wanted to know where Ronald was.

Q: And what did you tell him?

A: At that particular moment, I thought he was still in the house. And then when I looked in the porch, he was not, and I called up the precinct. They said he was at the First.

Q: What did you tell that individual?

A: I told him that he was at the First Precinct and I would make a call.

THE COURT: What did you tell the person who you spoke to at the First Precinct?

THE WITNESS: I said that a friend of the family, who is

a lawyer, wants to see Mr DeFeo. I told him he was at the First Precinct, and then he had left to go to Homicide Squad, which is in Hauppauge.

Q: Isn't it a fact that this individual who identified himself as an attorney to you actually went to the First Squad and then returned to tell you that Ronnie DeFeo wasn't there?

A: I don't know. I don't recall, sir.

Q: Were you told up to that point that reason why Ronald DeFeo was taken to the First Squad or to the Homicide Squad headquarters in Hauppauge?

A: That they were going to take a statement because it was too much confusion at the Ireland house.

Redirect Examination By Mr Sullivan:

Q: Did he ever tell you why he wanted to talk to DeFeo?

A: He wanted to ask him what happened, period.

Q: At that point in time was Ronald DeFeo a suspect in any criminal activity?

A: No, sir.

Q: Did this individual ask you whether or not he was?

A: No, he did not.

Sgt Gerard Gozaloff, Shield 526, assigned to the uniform Division of the Third Precinct, Suffolk County

Police Department, called as a witness in behalf of the People, having been first duly sworn, testified as follows:

DIRECT EXAMINATION BY MR SULLIVAN:

Q: Now, Detective Gozaloff, having obtained the Ireland residence as a command post, as you have testified, what is the next thing that you did?

A: Well, I had also been assigned by Sergeant Barylski to interview the sole surviving member of the family, Ronald DeFeo. And at this time Detective Randazzo brought Ronald DeFeo to the Ireland residence.

Q: What did he say?

A: He said that we had his full cooperation. He said he wanted to help us out in every way he could, but he was afraid. And so in line with that he agreed to go to the First Precinct and do whatever was necessary. We got in the car. When I had spoken to him about cooperation he said, 'Call me Butch.' So from that point on I referred to him as Butch.

Q: At that time what was Ronald DeFeo's apparent emotional state?

A: He appeared to have been crying and there was tears in his eyes when I started to take the statement and when I was interviewing him. But like he wasn't sobbing or anything like that.

Q: At that point in time was Ronald DeFeo a suspect in any criminal activity?

A: No, sir.

Q: And upon arriving at the First Squad at the time that you mentioned, where did you go?

A: They gave us an interview room which I entered with Butch and Detective Napolitano, and at that time I took an eight-page handwritten statement from Butch in reference to that day and the day before.

Q: I would like you to describe for us in as much detail as you can recall the conversation that took place during the taking of that statement.

A: Well, the first paragraph of the statement I had previously taken it in the Ireland residence. And after that we went into the day before. We had a discussion on the day before as to his movements, and at that time he told me that the previous day he had not gone to work because of stomach trouble. I asked him what was the stomach trouble, if he had ulcers, and he said he just had a queasy stomach, that he has to be very careful what he eats and drinks, due to that he had not gone to work. And he also explained that he worked for his father, who was the service manager of Karl Brigante Buick in Brooklyn, and that his grandfather Brigante was the owner of the agency.

And he said that he was up late watching TV in the sitting room in the house. And at this time he described to me where everybody slept in the house and more or less the layout of the house. And I had some difficulty in understanding him – as to where his mother and father slept and his sisters and brothers – because at that time I didn't realize that it was a three-story house. And I was getting mixed up with upstairs and downstairs. He would say that he slept upstairs, then he would say he came downstairs, but he meant like the second floor. And I thought he was down to the first floor. But then after that, when I understood that, he explained to me that his mother and father slept in one bedroom, and across the hall was his sister Allison, and next to them was Mark and John. And at the fourth room on that floor, which was the second floor, was what he called a sitting room. He said it was a small room with a TV in it. And he said that he was in the sitting room and that he watched *Castle Keep* on TV.

He said he went to bed. At that time I thought he meant actually in bed. And he said he watched *Castle Keep*. Then he said he had actually fallen asleep. He meant went to bed. It was in the sitting room. He had fallen asleep watching TV and that he had woke up about 4:00 A.M. and that he had a stomach ache. He said he wasn't really that tired because he had slept so much the day before. So he decided to go to work. And that when he came out of the sitting room, that by the bathroom on that floor that he had seen a wheelchair, and that he had assumed that Mark was in the bathroom, and that he had heard the toilet flush.

I had thought that the boy he was talking about might have been crippled and he was permanently in a wheelchair. But he told me that it was from football. He stated that they had a sheep dog that gets tied inside the back door. He said the dog is a good watchdog, and that he stays tied up inside the back door because the dog, as he put it, would shit on the floor. And he didn't get along with the dog too good. He showed me a bite on his arm. He said the dog had bitten him a couple of weeks before that. And I asked him, 'How come the dog bit you, you know?' And he said that he was sneaking in the house with his girl friend, that he wanted to sneak her down the cellar to get laid, and that the dog jumped him because he was inside the door and bit him.

And we had a discussion about his girl friend. And he said that he didn't have no money for a motel, and that she didn't like to go into a car, you know. I asked him if he actually would go in the house with his parents all upstairs, and he said, oh yeah, after a certain time that nobody would ever go down the cellar. He indicated it was a finished cellar.

He wanted naturally to leave out the part about the girl friend. Which it was. Anything he wanted to do, I would agree to. Then we had a discussion about him going to work so early, and he said that he often did it and that he would sleep in the car if he didn't go in with his father. But normally he went to work with his father. And he said that in fact some times he goes so early that the guys at work kid him about it. He explained that that day, the 13th, his father wasn't scheduled to go to work because he had to take Mark to the doctor's in reference to his injury. He stated that when he got to work that there was a subject there that let him into the building by the name of Vito Diorio.

He told me that he left at about one o'clock, and I asked him, 'How come so early?' And he told me that when your father is the boss, you pretty much do what you please. He said he did the normal things at work. At first I thought he was a mechanic, but then from the discussion it turned out that he wasn't a mechanic. He just did whatever he was told to in the premises.

He said when he left work at one o'clock that he went to his girl friend's house, who is Mindy Weiss. He said that his girl friend was Mindy Weiss, and that he was over her house until about three o'clock in the afternoon. And at this time he said that he called his house several times but got no answer, and that he had also called them from work between twelve and twelve-thirty. And when I asked him why he was calling so often, he said that he wanted them to leave out his pay stubs for his probation officer. And I asked him what he was on probation for, and he said that he was on probation for having a stolen outboard engine.

He also wanted them to leave out a house key because he said he did not have a key to get into the house. I asked him how come, and he said that although he has a key, a house key, on his key ring, that he took his mother's keys; that there are a number of them that drive; and that he explained that the keys are in a constant disarray – whose got whose keys, what keys, or what. And he said that on the keys he had were his mother's, and that there was no house key on that. And that at this he said that his car, which was registered to his father, was a '70 Buick Electra, which was colored blue. And he said that he couldn't raise anybody at the house either from calling at work or the several times he called from Mindy's

He said that at three o'clock, after he left Mindy's, he went to Henry's Bar, which is at the Ocean Avenue Shopping Center in Amityville, and that he had gotten there about ten after three. He said he had a Vodka and Seven-Up at that time, and then all together he had about four or five of them. I asked him why didn't he go home and break in the home if he didn't have the keys. He explained to me that he had done that twice prior, and that the first time he got yelled at, and at the second time his father had actually given him a beating for it. And this is why he didn't want to break in the house, because he was afraid of his father.

Later on, while I was taking the statement, I was having trouble understanding him. It seemed disjointed. He was jumping back and forth. I knew he was upset. And I thought that he might be a little drunk from following his movements from drinks that day. I didn't mean to hurt his feelings, but I asked him if he would take a blood test to see how drunk he was. And he got a little insulted. He said no. And at that this time he said, well, that he did want to cooperate, and that the reason he didn't want to take a blood test was because he had shot heroin that day. And he explained that he wasn't an addict, that he was a chippy shooter. Saturday night shooter, that he just shot once in a while.

Q: Now, what, if anything, was done upon the defendant's completing reading the statement?

A: When he completed and read the statement, I asked if he agreed with it, if there was anything he wanted to add, if there was anything he wanted to cross out, and he said no, that that statement was accurate. At this time I asked him if he would initial all the mistakes or where there were words added, et cetera, if he would put his initials at the end of the line, and if he would sign each page of the statement. And I explained the stamp to him, that I told him that as the stamp reads, that it's a misdemeanor if anything in here was not true. And I explained to him that that was in there because some people don't believe in God. So it's against the law even if you don't believe in God. And he initialed the mistakes and he signed each page of the statement, and I signed each page of the statement as a witness to it.

Q: What, if anything further, was discussed with the defendant?

A: We discussed with him if he would come over to headquarters with us. And also we discussed safety precautions because he seemed to be getting more frightened of this Mr M.; that he was convinced now that it was Mr M. who had done it, and that Mr M. had missed him because he had left the house early, and that he was frightened. And he said that he would stick close to us. He wanted to find out what was going on.

Q: At that point in time was Ronald DeFeo a suspect?

A: No, sir.

Q: From your knowledge of the investigation as it existed as of that time, were there any suspects?

A: Just this Mr M.

Q: Did there come a time when you left Ronald DeFeo?

A: Yes, sir. I returned to the scene of the crime. I walked through the house. I checked the locks on the door the way he explained them in the statement. And as he said, if you did not have a key and the door was locked, the way it was that it would have to be locked from the inside or the outside with a key. I looked through the upstairs room, and at that time the only two bodies that were still remaining were in the bedroom, Mark and John. I also went inside the kitchen where there was a broken window in a kitchen window, and it was ascertained that this window had fallen by itself while the First Squad was present and had actually been intact upon their arrival.

Q: After this inspection at the scene of the crime, what did you do?

A: I spoke to a Mike Brigante, who told me he was the mother's father. I asked Mike Brigante what his opinion of the thing was, and he said that he didn't know. I asked him if he knew a man named Mr M., and he said he did, that Mr M. was one of the most wonderful men that he had ever met. I asked him if he thought Mr M. would do that. He appeared to me to become insulted that I would ask such a question. I asked him if he thought maybe Butch did it, and he got even more insulted. He said he was a wonderful grandson, that he was proud of him.

Q: At that point what did you do?

A: At this time I turned to Rocco DeFeo, who had been standing about ten feet away, and just – Rocco DeFeo just yelled shut up to everybody present. He said words to the effect that this is family, don't tell him nothing. When he said this, everybody shut up. And it appeared that he was the boss. He didn't say much, but when he said it, that was it.

Q: What's the next thing that you did?

A: At that time I was assigned to take a statement from a neighborhood youth, number 100 Ocean Avenue, in reference to a dog barking.

AFTER RECESS

(Court reconvened at 12:20 p.m.)

SGT GERARD GOZALOFF, recalled as a witness, having been previously duly sworn, resumed the stand, and testified further as follows:

Q: And tell us what happened from that point on?

A: I went to the Fourth Squad, and at that time a number of different subjects were discussed with Butch. And I asked him about the dog. And he said that he hadn't heard the dog. And I asked him about what appeared to be the chewed part inside the garbage shed, and he said that the dog had done that several days before. That Detective Harrison had a discussion with him in reference to the guns in the house. He went over the guns that were in the house. Butch said that his father had as punishment taken all of his guns away. And he described them all, except there was one he said that he couldn't remember and that he wasn't even sure what caliber it was. He did not know what caliber it was and he didn't even know how to work it, that when he had first gotten it several years before that he was fooling around with it over a friend's house, and that the gun had actually discharged in the living room of the house and that the bullet had gone into the floor.

Q: Was there any other topics or discussions had during the course of this time?

A: He said that he hated the dog and that the dog hated him; and that he would lay in bed at night and think of ways that he could get rid of the dog. That he thought of running him over or, you know. And he said that his father must have sensed it because his father told him, 'Whatever happens to the dog happens to you. That if the dog goes in the canal, you go in the canal.'

Just before we left the Fourth Squad we had a discussion with him on what he was going to do. I had a discussion with him in reference to identification of the bodies. I explained the procedure to him that the member of the family has to identify the bodies in the morning. He didn't want to do it. He was reluctant. And I told him that I understood this, but I said as the sole surviving member he should do it, even though this Vinnie Procita would probably do it if he didn't want to. He said no, if it was his place, that he would do it.

And he seemed to be getting more afraid of Mr M. all the time, and he was more sure in his own mind that Mr M. did it. And he was getting scared. He said that it had to be Mr M. because he didn't think anybody in the DeFeo family would do that to their own, or in the Brigante family.

Q: When for the next time did you have any discussion with Ronald DeFeo?

A: The next time was at nine o'clock in the morning.

Q: Would you tell us what, if anything, occurred

concerning this investigation between 3:00 A.M. and 9:00 A.M.?

A: Between 3:00 A.M. and 9:00 A.M. we learned certain things, one of which was that it appeared at that time, although it was not completely definite, that all of the death bullets were .35 caliber, and that they all came from a Marlin made rifle. I interviewed one Robert Kelske who he had mentioned. I asked him about the guns that had been taken away, and he said that them guns had been taken away from him by his father for only a short period; that they had been in the trunk of his father's car, and that they were returned to him. I asked him if he knew all the calibers and everything, and he says no, but Butch did. Butch knew them guns inside out and upside down, and that he was a gun buff.

Q: Detective Gozaloff, did there come a time between 3:00 A.M. and 9:00 A.M. when Ronald DeFeo became a suspect.

A: Yes, sir. There was a discussion held based on the information that we received from Kelske and on the fact that we had the Marlin box in his room, and also that all the bullets were thought to come from a .35 caliber Marlin rifle. Discussion was held, and we all agreed that Ronald DeFeo was a suspect in this matter.

Q: What time did that occur?

A: This discussion took place about half past five, six o'clock. When we came back, Detective Harrison said that he was going to wake up the defendant, and upon his awakening he was going to advise him of his rights.

Q: What time was that?

A: That was at nine o'clock.

Q: What's the next thing that happened?

A: Detective Harrison and Detective Napolitano went into the file room, and Detective Harrison woke up the defendant. Detective Harrison told him that, 'Butch, you are the guy we are looking for.' He told him that he had the right to remain silent. He asked him if he understood it. He said, 'Yeah.' He says, 'Do you waive it?' He said, 'Yeah.' And he was protesting that he was here to help us, and George said, 'I'm advising you of your rights.' But he kept insisting he was here to help us. And Detective Harrison told him that 'You have the right to a lawyer, right now before any questioning, if you wish one.' He asked him if he waived that right. He said, 'Yes.' He was protesting all the time that he didn't do it, that it was Mr M. He told him if he could not afford to hire a lawyer, that one would be furnished to represent him before any questioning, and that the lawyer would be present. At this time food and some type of drink was bought. I had coffee. The defendant had something. Then Detective Harrison took him to the bathroom. He came back from the bathroom, he sat down on the cot again. Detective Harrison and I were in the room. Detective Harrison left the room and came in with two gun boxes.

He asked him if he recognized them, and Butch said that he recognized the .22 caliber rifle box but he did not recognize the .35 caliber rifle box. George told him, 'It was in your bedroom.' And he said, 'Gee, that might be the missing one, but that's been there for years since before my father took my guns, you know.' And George says – told him at this time – that the death bullets were .35 caliber, that they had come from a Marlin rifle, and that he had a Marlin box in his closet; and that Kelske had said that he got all his guns back; and that also we had reason to believe he was a gun buff and he knew the caliber of every gun that he ever owned. At this time I said, 'Butch, let's start over at the beginning.'

THE COURT: Was he free to leave the room or was he in custody?

THE WITNESS: He was free to go. We would have detained him if he went to leave.

AFTERNOON SESSION

(Court reconvened at 2:00 p.m.)

SGT GERARD GOZALOFF, recalled as a witness, having been previously duly sworn, resumed the stand, and testified further as follows:

CROSS-EXAMINATION BY MR WEBER:

Q: In your official report did you set forth any oral admissions that Ronnie DeFeo had made after 9:00 A.M. of November 14th, 1974?

A: No, sir, I don't believe so.

THE COURT: Did you make a separate report as to those statements?

THE WITNESS: No, sir.

Q: Did you know during the time of taking this statement that Ronnie DeFeo had a criminal record?

A: When he told me while I was taking the statement.

Q: What time did Ronnie DeFeo sign this statement?

A: He signed it approximately at 20 minutes after ten, 25 minutes after ten.

Q: Your testimony was that at nine o'clock A.M. Ronnie DeFeo was told that he was a suspect in the crime?

A: Yes.

Q: When was he booked?

A: 9:45 P.M. on the 14th.

DET. GEORGE HARRISON, Shield 319, Suffolk County Police Department, called as a witness in behalf of the People, having been first duly sworn, testified as follows:

DIRECT EXAMINATION BY MR SULLIVAN:

Q: What time did you see Ronald DeFeo at the First Squad?

A: It was about 10:30.

Q: What did you say to him and what did he say to you?

A: I introduced myself to him and I told him I was Detective Harrison, that I was with the Homicide Squad, that I was assigned to the investigation. He said, 'Hello.' He says, 'I hope you find out who did it.'

Q: At that time did you observe his apparent emotional state?

A: At that time he seemed composed.

Q: Is there anything else that you can now recall that was discussed?

A: In trying to demonstrate that he was being truthful, he did relate several incidents, one of which was a burglary that he had done next door with Kelske. He stated it was an empty house, and they were going to have an antique sale at a particular day, and the night before he and Kelske went in and stole some of the antiques. And he stated once before that, as he put it, he had loused up his father's engine in his boat, and his father told him to take care of it. So he took the boat out in the bay and burned it, and his father collected the insurance. He did comment that his father had a special phone installed in the house no one knew the number to. And the reason for this was his father could never get a call in. The line was always busy. And in this manner he could call home whenever he wanted to.

Q: Did you observe the apparent emotional state of the defendant during the course of this period of 1:30 to 2:30?

A: Well, he was becoming rather drawn, tired, and he appeared he had been through a lot, which he had. We asked him if he wanted to get some rest or lie down, or whatever, and he said he would like to, but he didn't know where to go. And he said he'd like to stay close to the investigation. At that time we volunteered if he wanted to go to the homicide office, that he had a cot there.

Q: To the best of your recollection, what time was it that he retired on the cot?

A: About three o'clock, sir.

Q: Now, did you thereafter occasionally check Ronald DeFeo as he lay in that room?

A: I did.

Q: And how did you do that?

A: Well, the door wasn't shut tightly, and you could open the door and look in on him. And whenever I did he was always lying down and always appearing to be sleeping.

Q: Did there come a point when Ronald DeFeo became a suspect?

A: Yes, sir.

Q: What time was that?

A: That was about six o'clock in the morning, sir.

Q: Between six o'clock in the morning and 9:00 A.M., what did you do?

A: Part of the time, Detective Gozaloff and I had left to go home to freshen up, and that was about seven, seven-thirty and we returned about a quarter of nine. DeFeo was still sleeping when I returned. I went into the back room and I woke him up. I woke him up, and he immediately asked me if we found Mr M. yet. He says, 'Did you find out where he is?' I said, 'Ronnie, we got guys out on the street looking for him, but to tell you the truth, I think it's you we want, not Mr M.' At that point he became excited. He said, 'What, are you kidding me?' He said, 'I'm trying to help you guys.' He said, 'You find Mr M., you'll have the guy who did it.' And several minutes have passed now. It was obvious that he was awake at that time. I said, 'Ronnie, I'd like you to be quiet. I'd like you to listen to me. I want to advise you of your rights.' I removed the rights card from my shield case, I sat on a chair directly in front of him, and read the card directly to him. I was no more than two feet away from him. Probably closer. I said, 'Ronnie, I'm going to read you your rights. I want you to listen very carefully.' He said, 'You don't have to do that.' I said, 'I want to read them to you. Now listen. 'I said, 'Ronnie, you have the right to remain silent. Do you understand that right?' He said, 'Yeah. I told you you don't have to do it. Don't worry about it.' I said, 'Ronnie, do you understand me?' He said, 'Yeah, I understand you.' I said, 'You waive that right?' He says, 'Yeah, yeah, I waive that right.' I said, 'Ronnie, anything you say can and will be used against you in a court of law.' I said, 'Did you understand me, Ronnie?' He said, 'Yeah, I understand, but I told you get Mr M. He's the guy.' I said, 'Ronnie, you understood me?' He says, 'Yeah.' I said, 'Do you want to waive that right?' He says, 'Yeah.' I said, 'Ronnie, you have the right to talk to a lawyer, right now, and have him present with you while you are being questioned. Do you understand me, Ronnie?' He said, 'I don't need a lawyer. I told you that.' I said, 'Ronnie, do you understand me?' He said, 'Yes, I do.' He said yeah, he didn't say yes. I said, 'You wish to waive that right, Ronnie?' He said, 'Yeah.' I said, 'Ronnie, if you cannot afford to hire a lawyer one will be furnished to represent you before any questioning, if you wish one.' He said, 'I told you I don't need a lawyer.' I said, 'Ronnie, having these rights in mind, do you wish to talk to us now without a lawyer?' He said, 'Yeah, I'll talk to you. I told you I'll help you all I can. I don't need a lawyer.' At that point I went into the room with the two boxes that I got from Detective Shirvell a few hours earlier.

Q: Are you referring to the boxes that apparently had contained weapons?

A: Yes, sir. I held the boxes up and I showed them to Ronnie. I said, 'Ronnie, do you recognize these boxes? Do you want to tell us about them?' He said, 'Yeah. That one box,' he said, 'I got a .22 rifle.' He said, 'That's mine, he said, 'but the other one I don't know.' He says, 'I'm not sure.' He was vague.

CROSS-EXAMINATION BY MR WEBER:

Q: Were you notified sometime that evening that an attorney was seeking to speak with Ronnie DeFeo?

A: No, sir, I was not.

Q: When for the first time did you learn that an attorney was looking to speak to Ronnie DeFeo?

A: I'll be honest. I don't ever recall hearing that an attorney was ever looking for Ronald DeFeo to speak to him.

Q: Is this afternoon the first time you have ever heard that?

A: Yes, sir.

Q: I'd like you to repeat for us once more the facts that developed between three o'clock in the morning and six o'clock in the morning that led you and the other detectives to conclude that Ronnie DeFeo should now be considered a suspect.

A: I learned that Detective Sergeant Della Penna of the ballistics section of the lab had determined or felt quite strongly that the weapon used in the murders was a .35 caliber Marlin rifle. I learned that Bobby Kelske had stated that Ronnie DeFeo did have the weapons back that his father had taken from him, as opposed to Ronnie saying he never got them back. I learned from Kelske also that Ronnie DeFeo was involved in a burglary at his grandfather's place of business; that a gun box indicating it did contain at one time a .35 caliber Marlin rifle was found in Ronnie DeFeo's room.

Riverhead, New York
September 23, 1975

(Court convened at 9:55 a.m.)

DETECTIVE DENNIS W. RAFFERTY, Shield 417, Suffolk County Police Department, Homicide Squad, Veterans Memorial Highway, Hauppauge, New York, called as a witness in behalf of the People, having been first duly sworn, testified as follows:

DIRECT EXAMINATION BY MR SULLIVAN:

Q: Up until 10:30 had you had any contact with Ronald DeFeo?

A: No, sir; I did not. I went in to speak to Ronald DeFeo, accompanied by Lieutenant Dunn. I introduced myself to Ronald DeFeo. I told him my name was Dennis Rafferty, I was a detective assigned here with the Homicide Squad. I introduced my partner Bob Dunn. I told him that he was a suspect – I was very sorry to meet him under these circumstances of this tragedy of his whole family being wiped out. However, he was a suspect in this, and I wanted to advise him of his rights. I asked him if he wanted to contact a lawyer, and he said no, he didn't want to contact a lawyer, that he wanted to help in this investigation. I asked him if he would go over his movements of the day before, and he did.

I said, 'Let's start the night before they were found,' and he did. I said, 'Let's start around suppertime. What did you do at suppertime?' He hadn't gone to work that day. He had stayed home. He wasn't feeling well. He had a stomach problem. He said that his family had had dinner about six o'clock. However, he didn't join the family at dinner. Everyone else in the family had dinner, except him. He said that he hung around the house that night mostly watching TV by himself. At about 11:00 o'clock he went down to the kitchen from the TV room, which was on the second floor, and had some epsom salts for his stomach problem. He said he returned to the room at about 11:00 o'clock. He watched TV until about 2:00 A.M.. He watched a movie by the name of *Castle Keep*. It was an Army movie.

I asked him where his family was, and he said that his mother and father were in their room, an adjoining room, watching TV, to the best of his knowledge, and he believed one of his brothers was there also watching TV. He didn't know this for a fact, but he assumed it by hearing it. I asked him what time everybody went to sleep, and he said that he didn't know exactly, but sometime between 11:30 and 12:00 o'clock he assumed everybody in the house was asleep. He watched this movie *Castle Keep* until about 2:00 A.M., at which time he fell asleep. He stated that he awakened at about 4:00 A.M., and he had noted that someone had turned the TV off and the light in the TV room off; that he hadn't done that.

He said that he had slept on the floor in the TV room. After awakening at about 4:00 A.M., he went upstairs to his room. He went to the bathroom, he showered, shaved, and went to work, leaving the house at about 4:40, 4:45 A.M.. He said that he left early because he awakened. Normally he went in later. But that on this day he couldn't sleep, so he went in early.

He stated that he arrived in Brooklyn at about five after six. He had went to a luncheonette and had a roll and an egg cream. He stated that he went to work at about 11:30. It was a normal work day. However, he left work about 1:00 P.M.. He wasn't too pleased with his job there. He said that he didn't make too much money. His grandfather didn't pay him too much. He was only paid about, I believe he said, $80 a week.

I asked him how long he had been working there. He said he had been working there for the past months; that he had the job – he had to have the job to stay on probation.

After leaving work at about 1:00 P.M. he stated that he came back out on the Island. He stopped at his girl friend's house, met with her. He went to a mall. I don't believe it was the Smith Haven Mall; I believe it was the mall by Massapequa. The Sunrise Mall, I believe it's called.

After leaving there, he stated that he took his girl friend home and went back – went to Amityville. While on the highway he had met a friend by the name of Kelske. He had a short conversation with him. And then he said he went to a bar named Henry's in Amityville. He had a couple of drinks, and he left at about 5:00 o'clock or so, went down to his friend Kelske's house. En route he passed his house and observed the cars parked in the driveway, and the house was closed up, didn't look like there was any activity there, went down to his friend's house, and his friend was unavailable to come out. However, he had a conversation with him through a window. He left there and he went home. Upon arriving at home – I believe he said it was about 5:30 – the house was secured. He broke a window, I believe, a side window, and he entered the house. He said the house was dark. I believe he said there was one light on inside, the way he had left it. He went upstairs to his parents' room and discovered his father had been shot in the back – he had a hole in his back – and he believed his mother and father to be dead. He didn't see any blood on his mother.

He stated that he left at that point and he went back – he went to Henry's bar and reported to acquaintances that his mother and father had been shot, and that is his story.

Prior to that I had asked him if I can call him Ron or Ronnie or Ronald, and he said his nickname was Butch, and that I may call him Butch. Again, I asked him, 'Okay, let's go over this again, Butch. Let's start yesterday. Start at about 11:00 o'clock last night. Where were the other sisters and brother?' He stated that the oldest sister, Dawn, had taken a shower. I asked him, 'How do you know that? Did you see her in the shower?' He said, and I quote him, 'I seen that fucking thing on her fucking head.' And at that point Dunn said, 'Butch, how can you say that about your sister? She is just dead in the last 24 hours and you are saying a thing on her fucking head.' It seemed like a little incredible. And he said, 'Well, that's the way I speak.'

He stated that when he left for work he didn't have the keys to his house, and that's why he had to break into the house that night before. He reported that the keys were always screwed up in the house. When he was leaving he didn't have his keys and he had to use his mother's keys, and he got them from her pocketbook prior to leaving. Did he notice anything wrong with his mother and father? No, nothing.

After leaving the house, he stated that he drove to Brooklyn. He was asked if after arriving at work – he went to work, 'Did you call the house at all during the day?' 'Yes, I did.' 'You did call the house? Why did you call the house?' 'Well, I was supposed to see my probation officer that night, and I wanted my mother to get my pay stubs out so I could take them and show the probation officer to indicate that I was working.'

When he met Kelske he had told Kelske he was calling home, had called home during the day, and there was no answer. 'Why did you do that? Why did you tell Kelske you called home?' And there was no answer. 'Do you always tell people that?' 'No. Well, yeah, it would be normal. I just figured I'd mention it.' 'What else did you do during the day, Butch?' And Butch said that prior to going to Henry's he had gotten off. 'Gotten off' is a term that indicates shooting dope. He told me that he scored some dope from a friend of his.

I asked him if he was a user or an addict. He said, no, he wasn't an addict. I asked him if he had a chippy. He said no. Chippy is a small habit. He said no, that he didn't, that now and then he just got off.

'Did you get high today?' 'Not really. Didn't even have too much of an effect.'

Q: Can you described the conversation that ensued?

A: I indicated to Butch that his parents and all his brothers and sisters had been found in bed in their bedclothes. He told me he knew that. 'Who was the first one up in the family?' He said, 'Well, usually my father.' 'What time did your father usually get up?' 'About 11:00 A.M.' 'They are found in their bedclothes, so that indicates that it didn't happen during the day, don't you think?' And he said, 'I agree it didn't. It had to happen before that.'

I then said, 'All right, if you leave the house at, let's say, quarter to five or five o'clock, do you think somebody was waiting there between five and six before daybreak who saw you leave and then they went in the house and did this? He said, 'No, I don't think that happened at all.' 'Then it's fair to say it didn't happen after 5 o'clock?' He said, 'I agree. I don't think it happened after 5:00 o'clock.'

I said, 'We have eliminated now between 5:00 and 7:00 o'clock. We know it happened before 7:00 o'clock. We know it didn't happen between 4:00 and 5:00 because you were awake between 4:00 and 5:00. You fell asleep at about 2:00 A.M.' He agreed. 'Butch, do you think it's fair to say that it happened between 2:00 and 4:00 o'clock?' He said, 'Yes, I do. I think it happened between 2:00 and 4:00 o'clock?' I said, 'Butch, do you realize you were in the house when this terrible thing happened? Maybe somebody came in there to wipe out your whole family and they missed you. You weren't sleeping in your room; you were in the TV room. It's unusual. Maybe they never checked it out.' He agreed. 'But, Butch, you must have heard something. We have a lot of shots. You had to hear something. How about the dog? Did you hear the dog barking?' 'No.' 'Did you hear any shots at all?' 'No.'

At this time Dunn said, 'Butch, I think you heard something. I think you are ashamed to say it. I think you are embarrassed to say it. Probably feel your whole family was wiped out and you didn't do anything. You probably heard it happening; that you were afraid, you were scared. That's understandable. If somebody was there. But you must have heard something.' At this time he was quiet, and then he said, 'I did hear two shots.' I thought that was a significant admission. 'Okay. You heard two shots, Butch. When did you hear them?' He said, 'About 4:00 o'clock. I was lying in there on the floor in the TV room and I heard what appeared to be two shots. And I was scared. I just waited for about 20 minutes and then I left. I got up, I ran upstairs. I didn't go to the bathroom. I didn't take a shower. I just left.'

Q: Did you observe his apparent emotional state at this point in the conversation?

A: Yes, sir; I did. He had been quiet. He was crying actually at that point when he said he heard the two shots. He was crying. He said, 'Well, then I left and I went to work.' I said, 'Butch, you heard two shots in the house, you leave, you just get up, go upstairs, and leave after hearing two shots? You didn't go to check anybody? You didn't go to see if anybody needed help? Maybe they were wounded. Who knows what it was? You just get up and leave? I find that very unbelievable.' He said, 'Well, that's what I did. I got up and left.' I said, 'Butch, if you heard two shots, you had to hear more. There were more than two shots fired.'

At this point he said – and he was crying again – 'I did hear more than two shots. First I heard two shots close together, and then there was a hesitation, and there was a third shot.' I said, 'Where do you think those shots were in?' He said, 'I think that was in my parents' room.' 'Okay. What did you hear then?' He said, 'Then there was a little longer hesitation and I heard a fourth shot.' 'Where do you think that shot was, Butch?' 'I think that was in Allison's room. It sounded a little further away.'

'Then what did you hear, Butch?' 'Then I heard two more shots. Not as close as the first two, the very first two shots, but there were two more shots. It was a shot, a slight hesitation, another shot. I think that was John and Mark.'

'What did you hear then, Butch?' He said, 'Then I heard, after a longer hesitation, I heard the last shot, and that was Dawn.' 'How do you know that was Dawn, Butch?' 'Because that was the furthest away, and she was upstairs on the third floor.' I added the shots up. I said, 'That's seven shots altogether.' And he added them up and he said, 'Yeah, about seven shots I heard.'

'What did you do? You must have been terrified when you heard this.' 'I was scared shit.' He said, 'I stayed in the TV room for about 20 minutes.'

We could understand that. We were sympathizing with him at this point. I said, 'What did you do after the 20 minutes?' He said, 'I got up, I went upstairs, I got dressed and I left.' 'You just went out of the house? Now you hear seven shots, you now know your family is wiped out, and you just leave the house? You didn't even check them?' 'No, I didn't. I was scared. You should have seen me driving.' 'Why were you scared? The perpetrator had obviously left. You had waited 20 minutes. You heard no more shots.' He said, 'Well, I did hear light footsteps.' 'But you never heard them leave? So you were afraid this guy was waiting for you outside?'

He said, 'I just got out of there as fast as I could.' I said to him, 'Butch, I find it very hard to believe that you would hear seven shots – and I'm sure you were afraid – but that you would run out of the house so quick without ever checking anyone. You didn't know they were dead. Maybe they needed help. Maybe they were only wounded, or at least maybe some of them, or one of them was wounded.

He said, 'Well, I did check my mother and father. I looked at my mother and father's room, and I saw my father had been shot in the back, and I couldn't tell with my mother, but I didn't see any blood. But then I left.' 'Butch, you didn't check any of your brothers and sisters? You just went out the door after checking your parents?' He said, 'Yeah, that's all I did.' I said, 'Your whole family has been shot by a .35 caliber.' I said. 'How do you explain that? It's your gun they were shot with.' He said, 'No, it's not my gun. I haven't seen that gun since I went on probation. My father took that gun away from me.' 'But, Butch, it's your gun. How do you explain that?' He couldn't answer that.

I said, 'It's unbelievable, it's totally incredible that you would just check your parents and not your brothers and sisters and just go out the door.' And he said he did check them. He started crying again. He said he did check his brothers and sisters. 'All right, what happened? How did you do it?' He said, 'First I checked my mother and father, then I went down and I checked Allison.' And he said, 'She got it in the head. Then I went and checked Mark and John's room.' He said, 'They got it in the back.' He said, 'And John's toes were shaking. They were still shaking and moving when I was there.' Because I knew that he had to be right close behind at that point if he saw that. Then he said, 'I went upstairs to Dawn, and she got it in the neck.' I said, 'Okay. What did you do after you saw all these people, you saw your brothers and sisters?' He says, 'Then I left and I went to the City.' I said, 'Butch, that's no good. That's unbelievable. They have all been shot with your weapon. We know it's your gun.' And he started crying again. And he said, 'I know it was my gun. But I didn't do it.' 'How do you know it was your gun?' He said, 'When I went into Dawn's room to check her I didn't have any shoes on. I was in stocking feet, and I stepped on the rifle. I looked down, and sure enough it was my rifle, the .35 caliber. I figure I was framed.'

'What did you do then?' 'I knew I had to get the cartridges and get everything out of there.' I said, 'How did you know there were cartridges there?' He said, 'I saw one in Allison's room. It was like a gold colored cartridge floating in like a puddle of blood. And I picked it up. And when I picked it up I got blood on my hand and I wiped it on my pants.' I said, 'Butch, you didn't even know your rifle was used at that point. You found your rifle when you checked Dawn's room.' He couldn't answer. He was silent. He said, 'I went to my room, took a pillow case, but the rifle and the cartridge in it.'

He said he changed his clothes at that point and also

put them in the pillow case because he had blood on them that he had gotten from Allison's room. He also said there was two pillow cases, and he put a second pillow case in the first pillow case.

'Okay. What happened then?' 'Went back to Dawn's room. I got the shell that was in her room. I went downstairs to Mark and John's room.' He said, 'And I got the two shells.' 'Where were they, Butch?' He said they were in the middle of the room. He said, 'They got it like this,' and he described how they were shot this way, and he cocked the gun and then went back and cocked the imaginary gun and then fired another shot from the right to the left.

Then I said, 'What did you do after that?' He said, 'I went back to my parents' room and I knew there had to be three shells in there. I found the first one and I couldn't find the last two. It took me a long time, what seemed like a long time.' And he found number two in that room under the dresser. After he found them he said he put them in the pillow case and he left.

He stated that he then left. He got the keys from his mother's pocketbook and he left the house, went down to the dock or the water at the end of Ocean Avenue where he lived. Prior to that he also stated that he had taken a 30.06 rifle from his room. No reason. he took the 30.06, put that in the pillow case, too.

Now he has the two weapons, the seven cartridges, his clothes, the belt, and the second pillow case in there. He drives down to the end of the Ocean Avenue by the Shangrila Restaurant there and he throws one of the rifles in the water, in the bay, and he thought it was the 30.06. He stated, 'I was going to throw everything in there, but I just thought for some reason that the air would get in the pillow case and it would float.' He said, 'So I only threw the one rifle there.' 'All right, do you know where the cartridges are or the other rifle? What did you do with that?' He said, 'I know where they are. They are in a sewer.' I said, 'Do you know where the sewer is?' And he said yes, he did. He drew a picture of the sewer.

Q: What, if any, conversation took place thereafter?

A: I explained to Butch that there had to be more to the story. He had to know who did it or see something or see certainly more than he had seen. It was his rifle that was used, the .35 caliber weapon, the bullets. And he became quiet. He was quiet for about two minutes. And then he said, 'You won't believe me. You won't believe me.' And Lieutenant Dunn and myself both said, 'We'll believe you, Butch, we'll believe you. Tell us the truth.' And he said, 'I have been framed.' He said, 'I know it doesn't look good for me.' He said, 'I was in the TV room sleeping at about 3:30 A.M. when Mr M and another guy came in the room, and Mr M. put a .45 hand gun on his head and told him he was going to live with this.' I asked him, 'What did the other guy look like?'

He could not describe this guy at all. The man was totally, completely not descriptive, indicating to me that he couldn't describe anyone because it was imaginary. 'They must have made you shoot at least one of them or some of them.' He said, 'Yes, they did.' They made him shoot his father and his one brother. I believe it was John. And I said to him, 'Butch, how did they make you shoot your father who was first? And then your brother who was fourth or down the line?' I said, 'I don't buy that you just had to shoot one. I don't think they were there. I think you were there alone.' And he became very quiet and he was crying. I was sitting very close to him and he was leaning on me and he was crying probably heavier than he had cried all day long. I had also felt this crying was not that remorseful. At this point he was crying very heavy. I had him over on my shoulder. His head was actually on my shoulder. We were sitting very close. And

I said, 'Butch, I know there is something more to it.' And he was silent, and then he said, 'I just started and it went so – it went so fast I couldn't stop. It just started, and it went so fast I couldn't stop.' I said, 'Okay, take it easy.' He was upset. He was visibly upset.

After he said, 'It went real fast, it went so fast,' I said, 'Okay. What happened, Butch? Let's go over it nice and easy, nice and slowly.' And he stated that it was about 3:30 A.M. he was in the TV room. He had watched *Castle Keep* that was all through. He wakened about 3:30, went up to his room, got his .35 caliber weapon, loaded it, went downstairs, shot his father twice, his mother, then into Allison's room, shot her, then shot the two boys, then went upstairs to Dawn's room and shot her. She awakened. And the dog was screaming loud. He said after he shot them he went to his room, he got the two pillow cases. He goes back to Dawn's room, picks up a cartridge, goes downstairs to the two boys' room, get the two cartridges, goes to Allison's room, gets the cartridge. It was floating in the puddle of blood, the gold-colored, on a shag rug, picked up the cartridge, and that's where he got the blood on his hand, put it on his pants. Then he went into his parents' room, found the first shell cartridge and couldn't find the other two. After what seemed to be a long time, picked up number two and three; put them in the pillow case. Back to his room, changed his clothing. He then went downstairs with his pillow case in hand, the two weapons, the seven cartridges, the belt, the second pillow case, got as far as the front door, realized he didn't have the keys or there was a mix-up in the keys. He said that all was true. Put the pillow case down by the door, went back upstairs to his mother's room, got the keys to the car, and there is no house key on those keys. That's why he had to break in that night, by the way. That's what he said. He comes downstairs with the keys and exits the house, gets into the car, drove down to the dock in Amityville, dropped the one weapon he thought was the 30.06, drove into the City and dropped everything off in the sewer. And at that point I ceased my interrogation. I was certainly satisfied. Detective Harrison and myself took him out of that room and put him in another room where Harrison was going to process him. That was about 5:00 o'clock.

Riverhead, New York
September 25, 1975

(Court convened at 9:50 a.m.)

MR WEBER: Your Honor, before I proceed, I do have two applications I would like to make. Number one, is as to the psychiatrist. He did meet with Mr DeFeo yesterday, and he requested that he be allowed to see the defendant today between the hours of twelve thirty and quarter to two. I told him I would advise the Court. And I would respectfully ask that that wish be acceeded to.

Your Honor, last night a so ordered subpoena was served upon Mindy Weiss in East Massapequa, New York. I went to her home and her father answered the door with the copy of the so ordered subpoena in his hand and told me that under no circumstances was he going to allow his daughter to leave the house. I informed him of the legality of the so ordered subpoena, and I told him that I would advise the Court of what he was telling me this morning. And I respectfully request that the Court issue a bench warrant.

ROBERT KELSKE, Central Avenue, Amityville, New York called as a witness in behalf of the Defendant, having been first duly sworn, testified as follows:

DIRECT EXAMINATION BY MR WEBER:

Q: Did you see Ronald DeFeo Jr, on November 13, 1974?

A: Yes, I did. I was driving up County Line Road in Amityville and he was coming down, and he saw me. We both stopped, and I turned around, and that's where I saw him.

Q: Did you notice any unusual markings on his face?

A: None at all.

Q: Now, did you see him thereafter on that day?

A: Yes.

Q: At about what time did you see him then?

A: Three o'clock in the afternoon.

Q: And where was that?

A: At my house.

Q: Did you have a conversation with him there?

A: Yes, I did.

Q: Did you observe him at that time?

A: Yes, I did.

Q: Did you observe any unusual markings on his face at that time?

A: No.

Q: Did there come another time that day when you saw him?

A: Yes, about 6:30, six o'clock that night.

Q: And where was that?

A: He came into a bar. He was at the bar for a while, and he said he had to go home.

Q: Did you observe any unusual markings on his face?

A: None. None at all.

Q: And did there come a time when he left the bar?

A: Yes.

Q: How long was he gone?

A: From two to five minutes, maybe, somewhere. It was a short time.

Q: Now, would you describe what you – what happened when he returned to the bar?

A: He came to the door and he pulled it open. He said, 'Bobby, you got to help me. Please come. You got to help me.' And he was hysterical and crying. I ran over to him. He fell to the floor like. I said, 'What's the matter?' He said, 'Somebody shot my mother and father.' Then I called the rest of the bar, you know, other patrons that were there, and we got into his car and we left for his house.

Q: Did you observe the condition of his face at that time?

A: Yes.

Q: Did you observe any unusual markings on his face?

A: No, there was nothing.

Q: What happened when you got to the DeFeo home?

A: Well, I pulled in the driveway and I got out of the car and I ran up the steps and opened the front door, and they followed. I ran upstairs and looked in the room, and I saw his mother and father in the bed.

Q: Where was Ronnie DeFeo when you went into the house?

A: He was outside crying on the car. Pounding his fist on the car.

Q: What did you do after you observed his mother and father?

A: I went downstairs. They brought me downstairs because I was pretty shook up, and I went outside to him. I said, 'Who do you want me to call from your family?' Somebody else already called the police. And he told me to call his grandfather.

Q: Do you know the name of the first police officer who arrived at the scene?

A: It was an Amityville policeman. I forget his name. He's been on the force for several years.

Q: Did there come a time when Mindy Weiss came to the scene?

A: Yes, she did.

THE COURT: All right, call your next witness.

MR WEBER: Michael Brigante, Senior.

MICHAEL BRIGANTE, East 29th Street, Brooklyn, New York, called as a witness on behalf of the Defendant, having been first duly sworn, testified as follows:

DIRECT EXAMINATION BY MR WEBER:

Q: Mr Brigante, are you related to Ronnie DeFeo, Jr?

A: Yes. My grandson.

Q: Are you employed, Mr Brigante?

A: Right now, I'm unemployed.

Q: As of – or on about November of '74, were you employed?

A: Yes, I was.

Q: And what was your occupation?

A: President of Brigante Karl Buick, Inc.

Q: Now, Mr Brigante, do you belong to any associations?

A: I belong to the Elks Club, Police Benevolent Associations, et cetera.

Q: Mr Brigante, I call your attention to the evening of November 13th, 1974. Did there . . . At approximately eight o'clock in the evening. Where were you at that time?

A: In my room. I was watching television. I saw my son upstairs for a phone call came in, and he ran back downstairs again. Next thing I know, there was a phone call that Michael got on again, my son. I said, 'Son, just what is going on here? What is wrong?' So I took the phone away from my son. The man said he was a police officer out in Suffolk County. He said, 'Your daughter just had a terrible tragedy.' I said, 'Now wait a minute. What is it?' He said, 'I can't tell you. You have got to come out here.' I said, 'Look, I can't get out there. Please tell me what's wrong. I lived with cops all my life. I know what it's all about. Please let me face it.' He said, 'Your daughter and your family are all murdered. They are all dead. Will you come out?' I said, 'Yes, I'll be out.'

Q: Mr Brigante, when you arrived at your daughter's house, who did you see there?

A: I became crazy, counselor. I went up to the commanding officer. I asked him to let me go in and see my daughter and grandchildren, and he wouldn't permit it. I says, 'You let me go in to see my daughter.' And I started to go in, and about nine cops grabbed me. I know I shouldn't have been there. I know in homicides you can't go beyond the line.

Q: Mike, did you see any other of your relatives at the scene there?

A: Yes. My nephew by marriage.

Q: What's his name?

A: Richard Wyssling.

Q: And do you know at that time what his occupation was?

A: A lawyer.

CROSS-EXAMINATION BY MR SULLIVAN:

Q: Mr Brigante, did you have any conversation with Rocco DeFeo that evening?

A: Rocco DeFeo shouted over to me. He says, 'Mike, don't tell them bums nothing.' And I said, 'Rocky, this is police business. All I'm speaking is the truth, so help me

God. I'm only telling them what I know. I know nothing. I'm here. They are asking me questions about my daughter, my grandchildren, my son-in-law, my grandson here. I got to talk to them. There is nothing to hide.'

Q: When for the first time did you hear that your nephew Ronald DeFeo was arrested and charged with these murders?

A: I don't know if it was television or radio.

Q: How was it that you came by this information that Ronald had been arrested and charged with these crimes?

A: I think it was in the newspapers or on the radio. Either one.

THE COURT: Is that the first knowledge that you had that your grandson had been charged?

THE WITNESS: Was arrested, yes, was charged with six murders.

THE COURT: A relative had called you and told you?

THE WITNESS: Yes.

THE COURT: You may step down.

THE WITNESS: Your Honor, have I got permission to kiss my grandson?

THE COURT: Yes.

(Whereupon Court recessed at 11:30 A.M.)

AFTER RECESS

(Court convened at 11:35 a.m.)

MR WEBER: With the Court's permission, I would like to call one witness who is slightly out of turn in the sequence of events, your Honor. Mr Leonard Symons.

DIRECT EXAMINATION BY MR. WEBER:

Q: Mr Symons, what is your occupation, sir?

A: I'm an attorney and associated with the office of Hartman and Alpert, Mineola.

Q: Do you have a specialty?

A: I would say the specialty would be criminal law. I'm a former A.D.A. for the Nassau County District Attorney's office.

Q: Mr Symons, did you appear and represent the defendant Ronald DeFeo at an arraignment proceedings on November 15, 1974?

A: Yes, I did.

Q: Did you observe Mr DeFeo as you were talking with him?

A: Yes, I did.

Q: Where did this take place?

A: In the lockup at the District Court in Hauppauge.

Q: Did you observe Ronnie DeFeo's face at that time?

A: Yes, I did.

Q: What, if anything, did you observe about it?

A: I observed that his lips were swollen, and there appeared to be a small cut and raised area above his left eye in the vicinity of his eyebrow.

Q: Mr Symons, did you have a conversation with him concerning the observations?

A: Mr DeFeo indicated to me that he had been beaten upon the head, he had sustained bumps on his head; that he had been beaten about the body, about the back; and that he, in addition to my observations, had bumps on one of his feet.

PATROLMAN KENNETH GREGUSKI, Shield No. 123, Amityville Village Police Department, called as a witness in behalf of the Defendant, having been first duly sworn, testified as follows:

DIRECT EXAMINATION BY MR WEBER:

Q: Did there come a time on November 13th that you were – that you responded to the DeFeo residence on Ocean Avenue in Amityville?

A: Yes, sir; there was.

Q: Approximately what time did you respond there?

A: I believe I received a call at 1840 hours, which is 6:40 P.M.

Q: When you arrived at the premises did you see anyone on the outside?

A: Ronald DeFeo, Jr, and there were four other subjects with him.

THE COURT: Were you the first police officer, to your knowledge, to respond?

THE WITNESS: Yes, sir; I was.

Q: Will you describe the state in which you saw Ronald DeFeo?

A: He was crying and a little upset. I asked what the problem was, and there was a statement made: 'My parents were dead.' With that, I went into the house and checked the house.

Q: What did you do after you went into the house?

A: Well, Ronald DeFeo went into the kitchen and sat at the table with Mr Kelske, and I went upstairs to check the bedrooms. After I checked the bedrooms, I came downstairs and I used the dining room phone to call my Headquarters and inform them that there were four deceased at the time that I had found and they should notify the First Squad Detectives.

Well, almost immediately after that Ronnie DeFeo made a statement. He evidently heard me overtalking on the phone and he made a mistake – stating that he had two sisters also, and with that I ran back upstairs and I checked a bedroom door that had been closed and found a young girl's body there. And I seen a staircase that I thought led to an attic which actually led to another bedroom upstairs on the third floor, and I found another body there, female there. I immediately came back downstairs, re-called my Headquarters and advised them I had two more bodies. After that call I went into the kitchen. I stood there with Ronnie DeFeo and Kelske, and I think I put my hand on his shoulder and just told him take it easy. I just stood there and waited until our detective arrived at the scene and our lieutenant. Sergeant Cammaroto was the detective, and Lieutenant Edward Lowe. They just checked the scene and they came back downstairs, too, and which was shortly thereafter that the detectives arrived.

RICHARD WYSSLING, 67 Woodsome Road, Babylon, New York, called as a witness in behalf of the Defendant, having been first duly sworn, testified as follows:

DIRECT EXAMINATION BY MR WEBER:

Q: Mr Wyssling, what is your profession?

A: I'm an attorney-at-law.

Q: Now, I call your attention to the evening of November 13, 1974. Where were you at approximately 10:00 o'clock in the evening?

A: At home in my bed.

Q: Did anything occur at that time?

A: Approximately 10:05 or 10:10 I got a call from Dr William R. Piro, my brother-in-law, that the DeFeo family may have been killed. And he said they got sparse news, and he suggested that I turn on the news on Channel 5.

Q: Now, before we go into the events that occurred.

Are you related in any manner through marriage or otherwise to the defendant Ronald DeFeo?

A: Yes. My wife is Mr DeFeo's second cousin. My mother-in-law, my wife's mother, is the sister of his grandmother.

Q: You are therefore related to the Brigante family through marriage?

A: Yes, sir.

Q: And is Dr Piro a member of that family?

A: Well, Dr Piro was married to my wife's sister. So he has the same relationship to Mr DeFeo as I do.

Q: What did you do after that?

A: At that point I got dressed and went from my home in Babylon to Amityville.

The Court: All right, thank you, Mr Wyssling. Step down.

The hearing will be recessed until tomorrow morning at 9:30. The defendant is remanded.

Mr Sullivan: I have an application, Your honor.

The Court: Yes?

Mr Sullivan: If the defense is in a position at this time to announce that they will rely upon psychiatric testimony at the time of trial, I have had a doctor standing by to conduct a Rufus Lee examination next week. I would like to make arrangements as soon as possible.

The Court: I have been holding off asking you anything about that aspect until you told me the examinations are complete and you have some sort of a report from the examining psychiatrist. Are you able to advise me yet?

Mr Weber: No. Your Honor. The psychiatrist examined Mr DeFeo this afternoon for the second time, and I haven't spoken with him.

THE COURT: I'm going to ask you to make every effort to advise this Court by tomorrow morning what the situation is as to your client's intention to raise upon the trial of this indictment the defense of mental disease or defect. The People have absolutely certain pre-trial rights here. They are entitled to know.

MR WEBER: Your Honor, I agree with that. But am I under the impression right now that we are supposed to start an immediate trial right after the hearing?

THE COURT: My intention is to remain on this assignment as ordered by the Administrative Judge to the conclusion of this trial of this indictment.

MR WEBER: Well, that was not my understanding, Your Honor.

THE COURT: I don't care whether it's your understanding. It's my understanding.

* * *

It is clear from these records, that the authorities had a solid case against young DeFeo. Through the testimony of witnesses, and, more importantly, by DeFeo's own admissions, the crime was reconstructed in its physical form at least. By the time the trial was set nobody doubted that young De Feo had in fact pulled the trigger, that he had killed his entire family. The emphasis would now shift from the physical body that killed the DeFeo's, to the mind that operated that same body.

3

Enter the Psychiatrists

It was clear to the defense attorney William Weber that his client might plead insanity as defense, especially if he were to be unable to suppress the confession allegedly obtained under duress when DeFeo was first arrested. This proved to be the case and Weber turned to insanity as a possible plea. At this point, it became necessary to have Ronald examined by competent psychiatrists. To no one's surprise, the district attorney prosecuting the case for the people of New York, also insisted on a psychiatrist being brought into the case. There was always the possibility that the two pyschiatrists, working for different camps, might differ in their conclusions. This, too, proved to be the case.

First came Dr Harold Zolan, a psychiatrist who had been asked by the Suffolk County District Attorney's office to examine the defendant. Mr Zolan, it appears from the record, followed the traditional approach of determining whether or not the defendant was sane, both at the time of the crime and at the time of the doctor's examination. If nothing else, the question-and-answer game played here by the psychiatrist with the defendant, proves how fragile the entire edifice of psychiatry is, how little below the surface it sometimes goes, and how quickly it sometimes comes to conclusions which cannot be reached easily or sometimes not at all. However, let the record speak for itself as it is transcribed by the official stenographer for the Suffolk County Court, Jeannine Menichino.

* * *

EXAMINATION BY DR HAROLD ZOLAN:

Q: How old are you, Mr DeFeo?

A: Twenty-four.

Q: All right, for starters, can you tell me who this gentleman is with the beige shirt and the brown tie?

A: My lawyer, Mr Weber.

Q: Mr Weber; do you know this other man here with the blue shirt?

A: Yes, sir, that's the District Attorney, Mr Sullivan.

Q: All right, where are you now?

A: In Suffolk County Jail in Riverhead.

Q: And how long have you been here?

A: Almost eleven months.

Q: All right, now will you tell me something about your earlier life, whatever you can remember of it, where you were born?

A: I was born in Brooklyn.

Q: And I know you can't tell me of your own personal knowledge where you were born, but were you told?

A: Adelphi Hospital I think it was.

Q: All right, now when you moved out to Long Island, where did you move?

A: To Amityville.

Q: While you were in school in Brooklyn, what would you say was the nature of your academic performance? In other words, how did you get along in school?

A: I didn't.

Q: You didn't get along?

A: No, sir.

Q: Tell me what you mean by that?

A: I just didn't want to go to school. I didn't want to learn. I just didn't want any part of it.

Q: With whom would you fight, the other kids?

A: Yes, sometimes I fought with the teachers, the nuns, whoever they were.

Q: When you say fought, you mean physically fought?

A: Well, I never hit a sister. I think I might have thrown a book at one of them.

Q: Directly at the Sister?

A: Sort of, but it didn't hit her.

Q: And overall, would you say that you got your way or they got their way?

A: I would say in the end they always got their way, but I didn't like it, you know, at the end. I had to do what they said, otherwise I would have left school.

Q: So, you finally gave in?

A: I had no choice.

Q: All right, now you moved out here and then I think you said in Junior High School you started Catholic School?

A: Yes, sir, I went to the Junior High School first; then

I went to Mercy in Riverhead; then I went back to St Francis Prep in Brooklyn.

Q: Why did all of this moving around happen?

A: I went to the Junior High School and they threw me out.

Q: Why did they do that?

A: A few times I blew up, just jump up for no reason, again with the books. I think I hit one of the teachers in the head.

Q: Are you right now feeling as if you might want to jump up and throw something?

A: No, sir, I don't feel that way at all.

Q: What would you feel like when you jumped up and threw a book?

A: It's no feeling. I could be sitting here and talking to you and the next thing I know, I could be hitting you over the head with a stick or jumping down your throat.

Q: It could even happen here now?

A: It could happen any time.

Q: Even though you're feeling pretty good?

A: Yes, sir.

Q: Then you went to where?

A: Mercy in Riverhead. It was a Catholic High School.

Q: And what happened there?

A: Well, my marks weren't that good. I wasn't into school at all.

Q: You mean you weren't studying?

A: No, sir, I was having constant arguments with the nuns.

Q: Where did you go after that?

A: They sent me to St Francis Prep in Brooklyn, figured the Brothers might straighten me out there.

Q: Well, how did you make out with the Brothers?

A: They threw me out of there too, sir.

Q: So, you left at the end of ninth grade, and where did you go after that?

A: Finally, I went to the Amityville High School. I was in Amityville and I did a year there.

Q: How did things work out that year?

A: Well, when I went there was trouble and most of the time I didn't go.

Q: In any event, at seventeen your father bought you a car?

A: Yes, sir.

Q: And then you went to work for your uncle?

A: Yes, sir.

Q: What did you do?

A: I worked in the store, delivered things, you know, sort of like that.

Q: How long did you keep that job?

A: Not long. I'd say about seven or eight months.

Q: What did you have against the kind of work that you were doing?

A: I didn't have nothing against that kind of work. I just didn't want to work.

Q: At all?

A: No, sir.

Q: Regardless?

A: Yes, sir.

Q: Mr DeFeo, you're in jail now and you are charged with a crime.

A: Yes, sir.

Q: What is that crime that you are charged with?

A: Murder.

Q: All right, now what do you think of all of that? You have been charged with what's obviously a very serious crime or series of crimes. What do you think about that?

A: Well, it's a shame. It's a waste what happened.

Q: What do you mean, it's a waste?

A: It's my family and you know, now they're dead. It's a terrible thing that happened.

Q: Did you kill them?

A: I can't remember certain periods of time in that night. Sometimes I think I did it and sometimes I don't think I did it.

Q: What makes you think sometimes that you did it?

A: I'm not sure. There's no reason for me to do something like that. That's why I honestly don't believe I did it. But it seems to look like I did do it.

Q: Now, you are telling me that you honestly don't believe you did it?

A: In a sense I don't see how I could do something like that.

Q: You say you don't see how you could do something like that?

A: Yes, but everything points towards me.

Q: A moment ago you told me you could see how you could do something like that.

A: Not the way I am now talking to you.

Q: What makes it look as if you did it?

A: The evidence.

Q: What sort of evidence?

A: The gun, all those things, you know, it's like a big puzzle. It starts coming back. The war picture I was watching on TV that night.

Q: What about it?

A: I remember watching that war picture on TV that night and I remember taking a shower.

Q: You mean, while you were watching?

A: I remember watching the war picture and I remember taking the shower but between the war picture and the shower I did something and I can't remember what I did.

Q: Now, would have have had any reason to be angry at your parents or your brothers and sisters?

A: No, sir, I loved my family.

Q: So, what you are telling me is that actually you believe you committed the crime but you don't remember doing it?

A: Something like that, yes, sir.

Q: Had you taken any drugs that night?

A: No, sir.

Q: Had you taken any drugs at all that day?

A: My mother gave me pills for my stomach.

Q: You know the kind of drugs I'm talking about, street drugs?

A: Oh, no, I didn't do any kind of street drugs.

Q: As I recall, you took a shower after you awoke on the floor?

A: Yes, I woke on the floor first.

Q: That's right, you awoke on the floor first; do you remember whether the television set was on or off?

A: When I woke up it was off and I don't remember shutting it off.

Q: Did you do anything else?

A: I don't remember driving to Brooklyn, but I remember getting into Brooklyn and going into a luncheonette and eating and going to work.

Q: Do you remember making a statement to the police at the precinct after you were arrested?

A: I remember giving that statement. I signed it, yes, sir. Just about one or two things that were in there that I didn't do.

Q: What they wrote is that you were over at this girl's house shooting dope?

A: That's the only thing I didn't do that day.

Q: Why did they put that down?

A: There was an argument, some kind of argument about me being a drug user and the people I was associating with being known drug dealers and dope fiends.

Q: You say there was an argument between you and someone else?

A: The police.

Q: But then you say everything else in there was what you told them?

A: Yes.

Q: But the statement that you make, are you telling me that they made it up and you said yes, or is this stuff that you actually told them?

A: I didn't tell them that I did it. They told me in words what I did and I seemed to agree with them. You know, like they might have said to me I drugged my family's dinner that day before, I remember the police saying that and I said no, I did not. I know I didn't.

Q: All right, now you say you had some recollections, you know, flash-backs about doing something with the gun. Did those flash-backs include some recollections of shooting anybody with it?

A: No, sir.

Q: So, to this moment you don't have any recollection of shooting anybody with the gun?

A: No, sir, I try hard, it's hard to believe; I have my family's pictures upstairs. I still, to this day, don't remember taking that gun and shooting anybody in my house with it. Like I said, I must have did it, but I can't place myself doing it.

Q: All right, tell me, what's the name of the President of the United States?

A: Ford.

Q: And the Vice President?

A: Rockefeller.

Q: Can you tell me the number of states in the United States?

A: Fifty.

Q: Could you tell me the last two states that joined the Union?

A: Hawaii and Alaska, if I'm correct.

Q: Who is the Mayor of the City of New York?

A: Mr Beame.

Q: Can you tell me, is there any similarity between say a banana and a peach?

A: They're both pieces of fruit.

Q: Have you ever heard anybody say 'A rolling stone gathers no moss'?

A: Yes, sir.

Q: Have you heard them say that?

A: Yes, sir, but I don't know what it means. I had trouble with the other doctor.

Q: The other doctor asked you the same thing?

A: Yes.

Q: Have you ever heard anybody say, 'A stitch in time saves nine'?

A: Yes, sir.

Q: Did he ask you the same thing?

A: Yes.

Q: And you don't know what that means either?

A: No, sir. I was all right before this happened.

Q: Before what happened?

A: Before I was arrested for this.

Q: Now, this thing, you know, this killing of your family, you said there's something wrong with it. What do you mean by that?

A: I said people that do things that don't have a reason for doing it, there's something wrong with them.

Q: I don't think you understood my question, Mr DeFeo. I'm asking you, regardless of whether you or anyone else did it, is the crime itself that was committed is there something wrong with that?

A: Sure there's something wrong with it; my family's dead.

Q: Why is that wrong? What makes something wrong with that?

A: It's my family. They had no reason to die.

Q: Suppose it wasn't your family?

A: I don't see why any person has a right to take another person's life. I don't believe that's right.

Q: In other words you say, are you telling me that it's wrong to kill somebody, to take somebody's life?

A: Yes, sir.

Q: And that if you did that, that you did something wrong?

A: Yes, sir.

Q: But you are still not sure of whether you did it?

A: No, sir.

Q: I see, but if you did do it, then there was something wrong with it? I say, if you did do it, then there was something wrong with what you did?

A: Yes, sir, if I did it, there's plenty wrong with what I did.

Q: Because it's wrong to take somebody else's life?

A: Yes, sir.

Q: Okay, well, do you have any idea now what may happen to you?

A: What could happen to me?

Q: Yes.

A: Get the rest of my life in prison, I know that.

Q: How do you feel about that?

A: I'm not happy about it, but if I did it, I guess I deserve what's going to happen to me.

Q: Now, you keep saying, if I did it; you made a statement to the police in which you indicated what you did and how you disposed of the weapon and how you disposed of certain other things.

A: I remember all that. I don't remember doing it, committing the crime.

* * *

But one psychiatrist does not make a case. William Weber, a skillful and experienced trial lawyer, had decided on a defense based on insanity at the time of the crime. Dr Zolan, on the other hand, felt that DeFeo was sane in the legal sense and therefore fully responsible for his actions. The questioning of the defendant had been a mixture of traditional proofs of sanity (some of it clearly bizarre in the light of the particular situation) and of questions relating to the crime itself. It is a moot point whether Ronald DeFeo Jr answered the psychiatrist's questions in a straightforward way, or whether he tried to feign insanity (if in fact he was able to). A person's character shows whether or not the answers are weighed by him.

Under the circumstances William Weber selected a psychiatrist with a wide understanding not only of the case and criminal justice but, as I was to learn later first hand, of the marginal ramifications of the case which most psychiatrists might dismiss out of hand. What follows is Weber's summary and his reasons for having his client judged not sane at the time of the crime. This summary was presented to the Court, and the pertinent portions of it are given in Weber's own words here:

'After consulting with psychiatrists who had examined the Defendant as late as October 13, 1974, defense counsel relied upon the defense of mental insanity pursuant to S30.05 of the Penal Law of the State of New York. Dr Daniel W. Schwartz, a leading expert in the field of forensic psychiatry, testifying in behalf of DeFeo, diagnosed his patient as suffering from paranoid psychosis, considered to be a major mental disorder. Dr Schwartz testified that at the time of the commission of the act, DeFeo, as a result of mental disease, lacked substantial capacity to appreciate the wrongfulness of his acts.

Dr Schwartz's diagnosis and opinion as to DeFeo's capacity to appreciate the wrongfulness of his acts was based upon testimony he read, upon the autopsy reports of the victims, DeFeo's Selective Service records, psychiatric transcripts of Dr Harold Zolan's examinations, letters written by DeFeo while incarcerated in the Suffolk County Jail, material as to the statement made by DeFeo to the police, and conversations had with DeFeo.

There were several important factors which Dr Schwartz relied heavily upon in arriving at his diagnosis and opinion. One was that despite the lifetime of violence provoked by his father, young DeFeo never physically struck back at his father. Dr Schwartz concluded that DeFeo was unable to deal with feelings of anger in a mature, healthy way. This inability to deal with feelings of anger was also reported by Dr Qualban in his reports made several years prior to the shooting.

Another important factor which Dr Schwartz termed 'dissociation' was that the defendant during the commission of the shootings, psychologically divorced himself (but not entirely) from a certain sensory perception of reality. Dr Schwartz explained that the Defendant had no awareness of hearing the loud discharge from the gun when he shot his father, mother and older sister but that the next day, he heard in his mind a sound of tremendous roaring in his ears. This factor demonstrated to Dr Schwartz that the Defendant was not malingering and that at the time he committed the crime he was in a paranoid state acting under a paranoid delusion.

Still another important factor which Dr Schwartz said reinforced his belief that the defendant was acting in a paranoid state and under a paranoid delusion at the time of the killings, was the manner in which DeFeo committed the crimes. Dr Schwartz recalled that DeFeo as a young man and for virtually his whole life, had almost no control over his temper. When he felt provoked and angry, he went into a rage, he tore up places. This anti-social conduct had no place in the killings of DeFeo's family. Dr Schwartz believed that DeFeo psychologically, unconsciously and unintentionally turned off his feelings while in the paranoid state and in an eerie, calm, machine-like way, he went about executing the closest people in the world to him, but the same people he believed were the greatest threats to his life. As Dr Schwartz reiterated, the striking strangeness in this case, was the Defendant's calmness throughout the killings. After the killings, DeFeo's conduct was such that on the surface it appears he was attempting to hide the commission of his acts. Dr Schwartz explained this conduct by stating that it was an action of someone who was just acting in another state of mind.

Also, Dr Schwartz discounted any robbery motive stating that Ronald J. DeFeo Sr's abundant source of money, which according to many witnesses, young DeFeo had access to just for the asking, would make it illogical for the Defendant to kill off this source of money. Also, to reinforce the psychotic thinking by the Defendant at the time he committed the acts, rather than any robbery motive, Dr Schwartz pointed to the fact that DeFeo killed not only his mother and father, but four brothers and sisters as well. Dr Schwartz stated that DeFeo killed his family because he believed that they, in some way, were a threat to his life.

Dr Schwartz said DeFeo was not hiding the murders from anyone, but that he just could not face life with the imagined blood on his hands and that it was just a neurotic, inappropriate act on his part. DeFeo did not appreciate the wrongfulness of what he was doing, and that he believed he was morally correct to save his own life.

Witnesses testifying in behalf of the Defendant in support of the defense of mental insanity, included relatives, friends and neighbors of the victims as well as the Defendant. DeFeo's uncle, Michael Brigante, Jr, recalled an event that occurred when DeFeo was only two years old. His uncle saw DeFeo's father, for no apparent reason, stand up at the dinner table and push young DeFeo into a wall banging his head or shoulder.

DeFeo related an incident that occurred when he was approximately 12 years old. His father, in a fit of anger, tossed a kitchen chair at DeFeo's mother, Louise. The chair missed Louise DeFeo, but struck the Defendant.

Despite this atmosphere of constant bickering, arguing and fighting, which resulted in DeFeo developing a hatred towards his father, the various defense witnesses uniformally agreed that DeFeo never struck at or physically fought with his father. As indicated in Dr Schwartz's testimony this was a vital factor in the development of DeFeo's paranoid psychotic state. Michael Brigante Sr DeFeo's grandfather, Michael Brigante, Jr, Phyllis Procita, the defendant's aunt, Mrs Lucy Burkin, an employee at the Brigante-Karl Buick Auto Repair Shop, Robert Kelske, Grace Fagan, each testified that in the face of his father's extreme aggressiveness, DeFeo never fought with him; he would either walk or run away from his father rather than physically confront him.

As Dr Schwartz described and as these same witnesses testified, DeFeo had a deep love for his family, including his father. Mr Brigante, Sr, remembers DeFeo as a good boy with a normal family relationship with his father. Grace Fagan told of an incident on September 26, 1974, where she was present at the DeFeo's house, for DeFeo's birthday party, together with the members of DeFeo's family. DeFeo, during the party approached each member of his family and lovingly kissed them, less than two months prior to his killing these very same people.

When DeFeo was 13 years old an incident occurred where he physically attacked his grandfather, Michael Brigante, Sr and his sister, Dawn. This incident together with the difficulties DeFeo was having in school, finally convinced his parents to take him for psychiatric counselling. Dr Qualban, at that time recognized the need for

DeFeo to find more direct ways to deal with his feelings. While Dr Schwartz stated that DeFeo, in his paranoid state, believed he had to act in self-defense, Dr Qualban, when DeFeo was only 13 years of age, recognized the growing fear DeFeo had of his father and he recommended that the fear of retaliation from his father be reduced.

In his middle teens, DeFeo used drugs as an unconscious means to escape his problems. The drugs made him oblivious to the violent family confrontations. After he discontinued using the drugs, his underlying problems with his father resurfaced, and increased. He tried to enlist in the army, but was rejected due to psychiatric problems he was having. On several occasions the defendant left his home, only to be threatened, coerced or bribed by his father to return.

Sometime in 1973, the love-hatred problems DeFeo was having as a result of his father's constant abuse of him and other members of his family, culminated in a tragic incident. DeFeo, unable to effectively deal in a mature way with his father, in an attempt to prevent his father from beating his mother, grabbed a shotgun, loaded it, placed it to his father's head and pulled the trigger. He pulled it a second time – the shotgun did not discharge. Unable to explain at that time why the gun did not discharge, and believing that a miracle had occurred, DeFeo's father, from that time on, developed an intense religious attitude. The Defendant, however, became psychotic and developed paranoid delusions.

Grace Fagan confirmed DeFeo's belief that people who knew him were out to get him. Mindy Weiss confirmed DeFeo's belief that everyone was out to get him. She described an incident at the Longfellows Bar, in Wantagh, where DeFeo believed he had been poisoned by an unknown patron or patrons.

While these bizarre symptoms were occurring, DeFeo

was described, by other witnesses, such as Lucy Burkin, as being kind, considerate and extremely respectful to them and other people.

As the fateful date approached, DeFeo unconsciously attempted to flee from his problems by leaving home; again, his father dragged him home.

On Tuesday, November 12, DeFeo did not report for work at the Brigante-Karl Buick Auto Repair Shop. Complaining that he was sick, he stayed in the TV room on the 2nd floor of the DeFeo house, adjacent to the master bedroom. At dinner time, he did not join his family but from the TV room he heard still another fight that his father was having with his sister Dawn. While running to her room, Dawn told DeFeo she was going to kill everybody in the house.

Later that evening, while DeFeo was still in the TV room, he heard his brothers and his sister Allison together with his father and mother in the master bedroom and he believed that they were conspiring against him.

As DeFeo remained in the TV room, in this paranoid state, he was watching a war movie called *Castle Keep*, in which several American soldiers were ordered to defend a defenseless position. At the end the soldiers are violently and brutally killed. Dr Schwartz pointed out that this movie, while certainly not causing DeFeo to commit the crimes, acted as a final catalyst wherein DeFeo, in his paranoid state, concluded that violence was the inevitable climax of all conflicts, and that he had to kill his enemies before they got to him.

A short while after the picture ended, DeFeo described a female resembling his sister Dawn, coming into the TV room, holding a rifle with black hands. DeFeo said he recalled taking the rifle from her, going into the master bedroom and pointing it towards his parents. He did not, however, hear any shots or noise from the rifle. He then stated he placed the rifle on the floor in his parents' room and went back into the TV room when he later heard several other shots which seemed to come from far away. He then saw his sister Dawn run up the stairs with a rifle in her hand. He then calmly walked upstairs to Dawn's room, saw her reloading the rifle, took it from her, pushed her on to the bed and shot her.

He felt an obligation to bury his family, even though he felt good that his family was dead.

The People Failed To Prove The Defendant's Sanity Beyond A Reasonable Doubt

Dr Daniel W. Schwartz, a noted forensic psychiatrist, testified that in his opinion, the defendant, as a result of mental disease at the time of the commission of the acts, lacked substantial capacity to *appreciate* the wrongfulness of his acts. Dr Schwartz's analysis of the evidence in this case presents a basis for a reasonable doubt, as the defendant's sanity as a matter of law.

The defense psychiatrist's testimony that the Defendant was malingering or fabricating symptoms must be judged within the nature of the crime and the manner in which it was committed. As Dr Schwartz pointed out, the nature of the crime was an act of insanity in itself. Also, if the Defendant was sane at the time he would have acted in the manner in which he was accustomed to act; that is signs of brutality and anger would have been all over the DeFeo house. There would have been signs of excessive violence beyond what was needed to complete the killings. Instead, the crimes were committed in a calm, deliberate fashion without any indications of brutality, anger or excessive violence beyond what was needed to complete the killings.

The best test as to whether or not the defendant was

malingering or fabricating as Dr Schwartz explained, can be found in the defendant's testimony which Dr Schwartz characterized as 'dissociation'. Dr Schwartz believed the defendant lacked the sophistication and psychiatric knowledge to fabricate his testimony concerning not hearing shots or noises from the rifle at the time he was shooting his mother, father and older sister, Dawn, but yet hearing shots when another person was shooting his two brothers and younger sister, Allison. This testimony together with the loud ringing in his ears, which the defendant experienced the next day and his continued telephone calls to his home in the hopes that one of his family members would answer, in Dr Schwartz's opinion was not malingering or fabricating.

Dr Harold Zolan, testifying from the People, in addition to stating that the Defendant was malingering and fabricating, stated that in his opinion, the defendant knew the wrongfulness of his act. Nowhere in Dr Zolan's opinion does he state that the defendant had the capacity to *appreciate* the wrongfulness of his act. As Justice O'Connor observed in *People v. Wofford, supra.*, a person may have surface knowledge of a wrong done, 'like the knowledge children have of propositions they can state but cannot understand,' but at the same time that knowledge can be totally without depth or significance and completely divorced from true comprehension.

It is clear from a reading of the record that the People failed to prove the defendant's sanity beyond a reasonable doubt.

> Yet one of the most striking facts about the abnormality of many psychotics is that their way of knowing is entirely different from that of an ordinary person. In psychiatric terms, their knowledge is usually divorced from all affect, which is to say that it is like the knowledge children have of propositions thay can state

but cannot understand; it has no depth and is divorced from comprehension.

The prosecution, certainly aware of the difficulty lay people have in understanding and applying the concepts contained in S30.05 of the Penal Law, capably and ably used the oral statements and the evidence from the storm sewer and Amityville waters in such a way as to lead the jurors to mistakenly believe that DeFeo attempted to conceal the commission of the crime, thus giving great weight to the proposition that DeFeo was not acting under a paranoid state.

Therefore, the relevancy and weight to be given to the following arguments is two-fold, bearing upon the evidence available to the prosecution to prove a prima facie case in the first instance, and upon the evidence available to the jurors in determining if at the time of the commission of the crime, DeFeo, as a result of mental disease, lacked substantial capacity to appreciate the wrongfulness of his acts.

The Legislature in new Section 31.05 of the Penal Law made a significant revision from the previous statutory codification of the old McNaghten Rule. The intent of that revision was to up-date the Statute in order to keep abreast of the growth in psychiatry. Psychiatrists have begun to devote more professional attention to emotional disturbances instead of purely intellectual disturbances. That purpose was accomplished by adding the words 'or appreciate' to the Statute. The Statute's intent is to exclude from criminal reponsibility those who have only a childlike comprehension or surface knowledge that their act was wrong, but lack the depth of understanding or feeling of wrong. The *Temporary Commission on revision of the Penal Law and Criminal Code stated:*

the fact that the defendant is able to verbalize the right

answer to a question, to respond, for example, that murder or stealing is wrong, or the fact that he exhibited a sense of guilt as by concealment or by flight, is often taken as conclusive evidence that he knew the nature and the wrongfulness of his behavior. Yet *one of the more striking facts about the abnormality of many psychotics in that their way of knowing is entirely different from that of the ordinary person.* In psychiatric terms, their knowledge is usually divorced from all affect, which is to say that it is like the knowledge children have of propositions they can state but cannot understand; it has no depth and is divorced from comprehension. (N.Y. Legis. Doc. 1963, No. 8, pages 18–19)

The statutory revision is particularly important in this case because one of the primary factors the People relied upon to show the defendant's sanity was that he displayed a sense of guilt by attempting to conceal his act. That was specifically one of the types of evidence that the legislative report said shows surface knowledge but not an appreciation of the wrongfulness of the act. Dr Zolan testified: 'If someone is suffering from a psychosis, whether it is a paranoid state or not, they may still have the capacity to know the wrongfulness of an act that they have committed'.

Dr Schwartz had stressed in his testimony that it was an appreciation of the wrongfulness of his conduct that the defendant lacked. In *People v. Buthy*, the expert witnesses for the defense similarly had testified that the defendant was unable to appreciate the wrongfulness of his acts, while the People's psychiatrist had stated his opinion was that the defendant had the capacity to know the nature and wrongfulness of his act. In those circumstances, the Court's charge that the People must prove that the defendant lacked substantial capacity to know or appreciate that the act was wrong was erroneous as a matter of law. Under that charge the jury was led to believe that the People had only to prove the defendant knew the act was wrong to find the defendant guilty. That is in effect the discredited McNaghten is standard.

Justice Stark's charge, in effect, gave the jury the McNaghten's standard. He failed to distinguish between the meaning of the word 'know' and the word 'appreciate'. The jurors, therefore, as in *Buthy* erroneously were led to believe that 'know' and 'appreciate' were synonymous and together stated a single criterion of legal insanity. Justice Stark's charge gave as that single standard the old McNaghten standard by speaking of intellectual understanding rather than the depth of emotional understanding required by the word 'appreciate'.

The error was compounded when the Judge, in reviewing the defendant's evidence on this issue stated 'he did not know the wrongfulness of killing them.' The Judge's failure to include the word appreciate at that point, was highly prejudicial, for two reasons. First, it was the most crucial element of the charge to the defendant. It was the summation of the evidence upon which the defendant believed the jury should find a reasonable doubt that the defendant was sane. Second, it re-enforced in the jury's mind the previous failure to draw a distinction between 'know' and 'appreciate' thereby further inducing them to believe the words were synonymous.

The Court Should Have Specifically Instructed The Jury On The Consequences Of A Verdict Of Not Guilty By Reason Of Mental Disease Or Defect

During the trial, the Court permitted testimony about

the consequence of a verdict of not guilty by reason of insanity.

The District Attorney asked the defendant, on cross-examination, 'Do you remember, Mr DeFeo, telling him, no, you're better off in a mental institution because you will be out in two years.'

In addition, a similar statement was elicited from a witness for the People, Vincent D'Augusta, in his testimony about a conversation between himself and the defendant.

Justice Stark, in his charge to the jury, stated as follows:

> Also, you will be instructed by me that one of the possible verdicts in this case is a verdict of mental disease or defect. Now you are not to consider any legal effect or consequence of such verdict within your deliberations. This is not of your concern.

Because of this misinformation, the jury should have been specifically instructed that should they find the defendant not guilty by reason of mental disease or defect the Court, pursuant to Section 330.20 of the CPLR must order the defendant to be committed to the custody of the Commissioner of Mental Hygiene to be placed in an appropriate institution of the State Department of Mental Hygiene.

In *People v. Adams* the Court held that as a general rule the jury should not be instructed about the consequence of a verdict of not guilty by reason of mental disease or defect. The Court acknowledged, however, that several jurisdictions hold to the contrary. The *Adams* court believed that such an instruction would deflect the jury from their primary task, determining whether the defendant was guilty. In this case, however, the defendant's alleged statement that he would be out in two years is central to the People's contention that the defendant fabricated his symptoms of mental disease in order to obtain acquittal. That statement would, therefore, inevitably be considered by the jury in the course of their deliberations. Speculation on the consequences of a finding of such a verdict would follow. The Court should have recognized that the inaccurate statements made before the jury would cause that speculation to be misguided. Because of that situation, only a full disclosure of the actual law in this area would prevent misguided speculation which quite possibly would influence the ultimate verdict because of the heinous nature of this crime. The Court should have realized that in this case the post verdict status of the defendant would be a subject of conversation in the jury room and surely the defendant should not be denied the possibility of an acquittal on the basis of mental disease or defect solely because the District Attorney introduced statements into the case that suggested the defendant might be out in two years upon such a verdict.

In *Lyles v. U.S.* the leading case held that the jury should be told the consequences of the verdict of not guilty by reason of mental disease. The Court presumed that the jury is aware of the consequences of verdicts of guilty or not guilty but the consequences of a verdict of not guilty by reason of mental disease is not part of the jurors common knowledge. There the Court realistically assumed that in any case the jury will consider the post-verdict status of the defendant in its deliberations. Here, that is a certainty because of the statements allegedly made by DeFeo. Therefore, Judge Stark's charge that the effect of the verdict is not of the jury's concern was an unrealistic statement of the manner in which the jury would deliberate. One of the primary reasons why the *Adams* Court held that the jury should not be told what the legal affect of the verdict is is to discourage such speculation. Here, fairness to the defendant necessitated not only a statement that the legal affect of the verdict is not of the jurors' concern, but a proper statement of what the law is even if it was coupled with an admonition that the post-verdict status of the defendant was not of the jurors' concern.

Obviously failing to understand the Court's charge the jurors requested that the Court repeat its charge concerning the defense of insanity. The Court did so and again committed the same errors as in its original charge.

Re-enforcing the defendant's contention that the Judge's charge to the jury did not adequately explain that intellectual knowledge can be surface knowledge, after the Judge charged the jury on the defense of insanity for the second time, the jurors returned to the courtroom to request the Court to be permitted to hear the testimony of the defendant in response to the question: 'If, in fact, you did commit these murders, would it have been wrong?' (Or words to that effect.)

THE COURT'S LACK OF EXPLICATION OF THE LIMITED MEANING OF THE PRESUMPTION OF SANITY WAS PREJUDICIAL.

Justice Stark's charge on the meaning of the presumption of sanity was as follows:

> Now, the common law of the State of New York contains the presumption that every person is presumed to be sane and to possess sufficient degree of mental capacity to be held responsible for his criminal acts until the contrary is shown.

The Court ommitted to inform the jurors that the presumption is a procedural convenience allowing the People to avoid the trouble of proving sanity as a material element of a crime in the vast majority of cases in which the question will not occur, and that it is a statistical generalization that most men are sane.

In *Brotherton v. People*, the Court held that once the defendant offers evidence tending to show insanity, a jury question is presented and 'upon this question the presumption of sanity, and the evidence, are all to be considered'.

A charge of that nature in which the presumption and the evidence in the case are stated together in the same paragraph adequately conveys the idea that the presumption remains in the case only to add weight to the evidence of sanity, and not to affect the allocation of the burden of proof between the parties.

In *People v. Silver*, the Court re-affirmed the principal that the jury may consider the presumption along with the other evidence in the case despite the forceful dissent of Justice Gabrielli who suggested that the word 'presumption' should be used only to define the procedural device of allocating the burden of coming forward with evidence while the word 'inference' should define the statistical generalization that the jury may properly consider.

Justice Stark's charge failed to explain at all what the concept of 'presumption of sanity' means and for what purpose the jury is to consider the presumption. At least in the *Brotherton* charge the presumption is put into the context of the jury's consideration of the evidence. Here, Justice Stark's charge is out of context and unexplained. The possibility that the jury will consider the presumption as somehow shifting the burden of proof to the defendant or giving the People a burden of proving sanity somewhat less than beyond a reasonable doubt is obvious from that charge given by the Trial Court in this case.

In *U.S. v. Hendrix*, Judge Van Graafeiland suggested that it is unlikely that the jury would be confused in attempting to reconcile the government's burden of proof beyond a reasonable doubt with the 'presumption of sanity' which suggests that the defendant has a burden of showing more than reasonable doubt in order to obtain an acquittal. Similarly, Justice Stark's charge could easily lead the jury to reach the same erroneous conclusion because it suggests the defendant is to be held responsible until the defendant show the contrary. The illogical insertion of the definition of presumption of sanity in the midst of the statutory definition of legal insanity is extremely prejudicial to the Defendant in that the Court failed to properly limit the scope of the jury's consideration of, and the weight given to the 'presumption of sanity'.

4

A Visit to Amityville in the Dead of Winter

Out on Long Island a lot of people have not only read my books, but have been students or friends of mine during the periods when I teach parapsychology at the New York Institute of Technology at Old Westbury, Long Island. Or they might have seen me on television. Be this as it may, in June of 1976, a certain Mrs Helen Ruland wrote to me concerning the house in Amityville which was then so much in the news. She said, in part, 'in December of 1975, the Lutz family moved in. They are George and Kathleen Lutz and three small children. The family was there 28 days and moved out with only three changes of clothing. Channel 5 News started to investigate it and showed film of the inside of the house. All the beds were unmade and the ironing board and iron was still up. According to the news stories, the Vatican sent two priests to investigate, and they in turn said there definitely was "something" in the house.

'I must tell you that before this story was written I had heard about it through my brother-in-law. He heard it from a friend who was discussing an annulment with the priest who investigated the house for the Lutz's. After telling the story to friends and family they all thought me crazy. Then it came out in Newsday, the Long Island Press, and on the Channel 5 News. They didn't call me crazy anymore. As you know, I am very interested in this type of thing, so I went out to the house. My husband James refused to go, him being an unbeliever; my girlfriend was afraid, so she asked her husband to take me. He, himself has never had any experiences with the supernatural, but he has an open mind. We went out there in the beginning of March. After being there for over an hour, we saw a thin white light at the left second story window. It only lasted two or three seconds, but we both saw it from the car which was parked at a perfect angle across the street. The house, of course, was in total darkness. After seeing this light, we tried to think of all the things it could have been. We discounted the glare of light because, for one, we saw an actual light not a glare. Secondly, after many cars going by, none showed their lights at any portion of the second floor. The house next door neither turned on nor turned off any lights. There was nothing we could think of that it could have been.

'On Wednesday, June 2, 1976 I went out there again with two friends of mine named Joanne Krut and Donna Lacey. By the way, it took me a long time for the fear which overcame me after watching that house to subside. I was so frightened I didn't sleep for a week. My feeling was that the house was filled and reeked with evil and that it actually reached out to touch me.

'As I said, my two friends and I went to watch the house again. We arrived at 8:15 p.m. At 9:55 Joanne's eyes started to tear. Up until then she had almost fallen asleep leaning against the door. We were all calm and not a bit frightened. About 10 seconds after her eyes started to tear, we saw a small pin-point of light flashing in one of the windows above the front door. There are six windows on the one side of the second level. The light was first in one of the middle windows then went to the extreme left window then it started from that window across to the five other windows. Once again we tried to figure out what it had been and again there was no logical reason for the lights. By the way, both the first time and this second time, I saw this light although the lights themselves were different, seemed to be coming from inside of the house.

'From reading your books I think you're the only person capable of ridding that house, along, of course, with a medium, so that the Lutz family can move back in. It is a beautiful house and should have a family living in it that can fill it with laughter.'

I wrote back thanking Mrs Ruland for her interest and confidence in me, and suggested that if she wanted me to get involved in the case she would have to bring it to the attention of the attorney representing either the DeFeo family or the present owner of the house. Meanwhile I had been approached by Channel 5, Metromedia, with a request to come out to the house which was then empty – the Lutzes having fled – to do a program from the house. At first, I was willing to consider such an enterprise, provided I would have had free reign and there would have been no time limitation. When I discovered that all they wanted of me were eight minutes to tell the entire story, to conclude an investigation that might take days, I declined. Nevertheless, Metromedia kept calling me and begging me to come out and I, equally firmly, refused to do anything I considered unprofessional. Earlier, in March of 1976, I had been contacted by a certain Stephen Kaplan who has described himself as a 'social scientist' in an interview in the newspaper Long Island Press. Dr Kaplan (I don't know what his doctorate is in) lectures on vampires and Dracula, and is a frequent visitor to various talk shows. According to the article in the Long Island Press, Mr Kaplan is a graduate of City College with degrees in sociology, education, liberal arts, communications and a healthy sprinkling of public relations, which apparently stood him in good stead, for the ever present Kaplan is also the executive director of the Parapsychology Institute of America, the Vampire Research Center of America, and the Ghostology Institute of America, all of which he operates single-handedly out of his Centereach home. Mr Kaplan was very friendly when he called and asked that I join him in an investigation of the Amityville house. I was equally friendly in turning down the invitation, not so much because I didn't want to investigate the house, now that it was empty again, but because I had some serious doubts concerning Mr Kaplan's various enterprises.

However, in the fall of 1976 I was approached by the attorneys for Ronald DeFeo, Jr, the condemned man, to work with them on the case in as far as the parapsychological aspects were concerned. An agreement was made for me to visit the house in the company of a competent medium. By that time the Lutz family had moved out and gone to California, and their account, dramatized in the best-seller 'The Amityville Horror,' had not yet become a reality. The house stood empty, and yet the bank, which was in charge of it was extremely reluctant to allow me to visit. Finally, William Weber and Bernard Burton, the attorneys in charge of the case, persuaded the bank to allow a visit after all. Mr Weber was then pursuing an appeal on behalf of Ronald DeFeo, Jr, and it was felt that any new evidence which might turn up as a result of my visit to the house, could be used in such an appeal. Consequently, there was no way in which the bank could turn down the request, and in the end it was granted. That visit took place on January 13, 1977, in the afternoon, on what was one of the coldest days of January of that winter, and perhaps any winter in recent memory.

When we arrived at the house, there was some problem with the front door at first, which could be attributed to the extreme cold of the day. Finally, Ethel Johnson Meyers, my venerable friend and a trance medium; a researcher from Channel 5 by the name of Laura DiDio and attorneys William Weber and Bernard Burton, entered the premises where so much had occurred only some 15 months before. The house was now totally empty and curiously bland. With all the furniture gone, the rooms seemed to be identical and yet one received different impressions as one entered them. As is my habit in all investigations of haunted houses, I allowed Ethel Meyers to precede me slightly and I would follow her. Not too unlike a bloodhound. Mrs Meyers then sought out the most active areas in such a house, giving at first her clairvoyant impressions. After a while of this I would ask her to select a good area, that is good from the point of view of psychic material, and make herself comfortable, or as comfortable as she could. I would then suggest that she allow deep trance to take place. For the moment, however, we ran up and down the stairs, looked into all the rooms and gathered impressions. From time to time I recorded her activities on motion picture film until my camera came to a sudden halt. No amount of opening and closing the camera, no pushing and pulling would make it work again, yet there was no logical reason why it should stop. However, I had experienced similar mechanical failures in other haunted houses due to the presence of electromagnetic fields in the atmosphere, and I did not pursue the matter further. In addition to our group, there was now present a woman whose talent was psychic photography. No matter where, no matter what was in front of her camera – usually a Polaroid camera which develops pictures on the spot – Gerri Warner produced paranormal pictures with it. These ranged from figures to amorphous shapes of ectoplasm, but were always of a supernormal origin. I asked Miss Warner to take pictures in every one of the rooms. To our amazement they clearly showed a kind of aura around the area where the bullet had entered the body of the victim. There seems to be no rational explanation for the presence of these auras, and as the pictures were developed on the spot and were taken with a camera in excellent working order, nothing but a paranormal explanation will fit.

At no time did I inform Mrs Meyers where we would

be going that day, nor what for. As far as she was concerned it was a routine investigation of a haunted house, similar to hundreds of such investigations she and I had gone to together in the past. When we got into Amityville, I'm sure she was not even aware of the name of the town, and when we arrived at the house she had no idea why she was there or what had transpired in the house other than what her psychic senses told her.

Immediately upon entering the premises, she began to talk and I recorded every one of her words, because it clearly indicates that she hit the psychic nail on the head. Her description of the 'problem' of the house, of some of the consequences, is entirely correct. Yet there was nothing that would allow her to connect the house with the Amityville murders, with DeFeo or the Lutz family, which by then had gotten quite a bit of publicity. I am always very careful to keep mediums who work with me from any extraneous knowledge concerning the object of our work, and in this case I am satisfied that I succeeded fully.

In the following I am presenting a complete transcript of the investigation by Mrs Ethel Johnson Meyers in the house in Amityville, located at 112 Ocean Avenue.

January 13, 1977

H: Ethel, what are the impressions of this house?

E: I'm getting an odor.

H: What's the odor from?

E: I don't know my head's cracked.

H: Head's cracked? Who's head?

E: Mine, at the moment . . . I have to get used to the cold for a moment.

H: All right. Are you comfortable?

E: Reasonably.

H: Where do you think is the center of the activities you feel?

E: Let me relax a little more because I have two shocks and I want to see where they lead to.

H: Okay . . .

E: Right up here.

H: We are on the third floor, the top floor of the house. The house is without heat. It's empty and boarded up. This is the corner bedroom.

E: You have a lot of Indians – burial ground here. Hmmpf. I feel as if I'm choked.

H: Is there any connection of that with the house?

E: I'll say.

H: What connection?

E: Whoever lives here is going to be the victim of all the anger – its blind fierceness.

H: Who's anger is it?

E: The Indians.

H: Any particular ones?

E: Secret. Seems to be one with a lot of feathers around, too.

H: How far back are you going?

E: There's one without any feathers at all, and kind of rough dress. And a long jaw.

H: Is this a long time ago?

E: The burial ground, yes. But they still linger.

H: Why are they angry?

E: Because this has been a sacred place – and this is over a very very special chief's tomb.

H: Do you sense them present in person or do you see it as an imprint?

E: I sense the one present, not an imprint.

H: An entity?

E: The one with the slung jaw.

H: Is he aware of you?

E: Sure is. He's giving me a bad time.

H: Would you try to tell them that we are respectful of their tradition and will do everything to satisfy them.

E: That is what (somebody) is saying. They understand.

H: That we're not hostile; that we have come to make things right. Not to be angry at us.

E: *Somehow a white person got to digging around and doing things and might have dug up a skeleton.*

H: Who got at the skeleton?

E: A long time ago and the white man is a heinous evil devil. My whole head is aching like mad – not because of the cold but . . .

H: I understand. Now, did they have any contact with any one living in this house.

E: I'll say.

H: What exactly happened?

E: Everything happens in here. When they are very mad everybody goes crazy. Somebody strangled somebody here? Because my throat seems to be closing.

H: Why did they do that?

E: *The whole atmosphere – people get to fighting with each other because they don't know why.* They're driven to it *because they are taken over* by the one with the long jaw.

H: And what does he make them do?

E: Fight and bang up each other.

H: Has he in fact done that to anyone in the house?

E: Yes.

H: How long ago?

E: I think it's been more than one. Strange things happen.

H: What sort of things happen?

E: Violence of death – my skull is cracked and my neck is stretched.

H: And how was this accomplished. In other words, who did it?

E: *The Indian force takes over* a . . . that which . . . um, I can't even talk.

H: The Indian force takes over . . . what?

E: *A psychic nature or a tender nervous system of an individual – usually a male.*

H: What will the male do under those circumstances?

E: Anything the Indian desires him to do.

H: What did this Indian desire?

E: My whole face seems to be battered in and my neck seems to be stretched. I can't get away from that.

H: What would that indicate?

E: I might have been hung.

H: *Did this Indian take over any male in this house?*

E: *I would say so . . . yes.*

H: What sort of male was taken over in this house? What kind of person?

E: A catalyst that could be used. I have to be a little quieter to get at that. I'm so high-strung at the moment – I don't know whether I'm the person doing it or the person being done to. I think I'm the person being done to. (noises – choking – coughing)

H: Is there a presence in this house other than the Indians?

E: Yes.

H: Who would that be?

E: I think it's this person. (heavy breathing)

H: Would you like to sit down somewhere?

E: For a moment.

H: We can arrange it. There are some pillows in here. Now how long ago did all this take place?

E: Is there an Emma or Emily?

H: I don't know. Do you sense such a person in the living or in spirit?

E: Somebody just screamed that.

H: How long ago did this happen?

E: There is so much time being thrown around here – like the ancient burial ground and the ghost of this . . . of this Indian with the feathers, the great chief.

H: Ask your people what tribe the Indian belonged to.

E: Swanee . . .

H: Now what exactly took place in this house? Can you get anything on the events themselves?

E: Was there also a child here?

H: How old is the child?

E: Seems . . . oh . . .

H: Is it a male or a female? (very long pause)

E: Good looking woman here.

H: How old is the woman?

E: Young. Hard to . . . right here.

H: What does she look like?

E: Good looking.

H: Is she alive or dead?

E: I don't think she's alive.

H: Can you get her name?

E: Not at the moment.

H: Why is she here?

E: A man with darker hair. Dark hair and eyebrows.

H: How old is he?

E: Youngish also, not an old man.

H: Do you get anything about him – his name, his connection?

E: He looks as if he might be a part of the Indian that does that – the Indian that takes over.

H: Did the Indian take over the man? Is that what you are saying? (long pause – no answer) Why is he taking over this man?

E: To commit a foul deed.

H: Who is planning the deed?

E: That Indian with the feathers is frantic because of his scalp being made a toy of.

H: His skeleton?

E: Yeah, but they didn't do it. It was a long, long time ago. But every white man is a bad man, must be destroyed. And it's not always everybody that they can control. This is a catalyst they *can* control.

H: Why can they control this particular one?

E: I said he was a catalyst.

H: Do you mean he was psychic?

E: Yes. He might not have known it but a lot of people are psychic and don't know it and are subject to . . .

H: What did this catalyst then do in this house?

E: I would say he destroyed this woman.

H: Can you tell me more what this person did once he was taken over?

E: A lot of strange things. Seems to wander around at night. I don't think it's sleepwalking but it's something under trance.

H: Is he aware of this strangeness?

E: No.

H: Is he consciously doing any of this?

E: No. Not in his consciousness, but it's like a trance – *when it takes over it's deadly*.

H: What does he do under the influence of this entity?

H: How many people are involved in all this?

E: I think it's down the years quite a few. But recently . . . I don't know. I got hooked up with this particular Indian and this man.

H: What is the result of this Indian's influence on the dark haired young . . . or old . . . you didn't tell us the age of this man.

E: Medium age. Not too young.

H: What is the result of this influence?

E: He's unreliable as to what he's going to do next.

H: Do you see this happening or is it an imprint from the past?

E: It looks like it happens right up here.

H: By up here, do you mean upstairs?

E: Well it begins here anyway.

H: What does he do again? How many people are involved?

E: You mean just now? *I think maybe a whole family can be involved.* It's very funny.

H: The whole family?

E: *Several people. I'm berserk.*

H: Then who's the person that runs berserk?

E: The man.

H: What does he do?

E: Oh, must I go into that?

H: You must. (very long pause) What does he do?

E: You see I have to suffer this myself and I was trying not to have to do this.

H: Yes, but how would you describe it.

E: I think there is a young fellow here too, but I'm not sure. (voice is almost sobbing)

H: What does the young boy do?

E: *He is a victim.*

H: How old a young boy is he?

E: *He seems to be very young, early teens or so, and a girl around that time too.*

H: The girl in her teens too?

E: Four individuals I think – four. Oh, I'm just trying to get around the corners to get away from it.

H: Now prior to these people coming here, has anybody else done anything like this?

E: Oh yes, long time . . . the surroundings here have had funny things happening to them. Because this house has somebody early – *not this house but another* – early people digging here. It was like a farm or something and digging here *they have come onto this skull and that starts the whole bit.*

H: What, another house on this spot?

E: Not on this spot but they were digging on this spot. *They built this house later* – much, much, much later.

H: There were people here before?

E: Yes.

H: Before this house was built? They were living on this spot?

E: This land. Yes.

H: What were they doing here?

E: Farm.

H: So there must have been a farm house.

E: Not right on this spot. They were digging on this spot and I think it was a young boy who dug and found that and *made a toy out of this skull and the Indian never forgot it.* Now he can't touch everybody if they are not vulnerable. But that boy was vulnerable too. And he was chopped up.

H: Now the boy who did it, was he also a victim of this?

E: Yes he was.

H: Do you sense him around here now?

E: Yes.

H: Do you sense any other people who were the result of all this in this place?

E: It's been a long history, and anybody who is psychic – *they are a victim*. If you are not with this type of thing that makes you psychic the chemistry is not vulnerable – you get by. You may not have such good luck. This has to be laid – this poor Indian who has his skull – he should be laid. *He's walking around.*

H: He's still here?

E: Yes. That has to be latter 1700's – maybe early 1800's.

H: Now do you sense this Indian present now as you speak?

E: With the feathers?

H: Yes.

E: I don't sense him in this room. They are showing him to me and he is around here and has been up through the house . . . but he is not the one who perpetrates . . . he just orders.

H: Who is the one who is responsible for what has happened here?

E: That took over the individual in the house?

H: Yes.

E: That one with the under-slung jaw. He looks like an Indian much later than that other Indian, but he is buried under there.

H: Do you sense him close enough to talk to him?

E: Well, he doesn't speak English. Albert* says.

H: Can Albert get through to him?

E: He's getting the Indians to get through to him.

H: Ask Albert that the house be cleansed of this for future reference.

E: He says with Lavangatong (phonetic spelling), with White Plume and the White Bull things can be straightened out – nothing in the past can be restored.

H: Well, ask Albert about this man who has taken over here and committed these acts that you have mentioned – whether there is something we should know that would help us.

E: Who's going to believe that a psychic force has taken over an individual in order to make them commit such atrocities?

H: That remains to be seen.

E: A man can be judged as insane.

*Albert is Mrs Meyers' 'control person.'

H: But suppose there is some information that can help us. We should try.

E: The best that we can do is simply say that he was a right hand of the fury . . . of past fury . . . beyond that. That until these things are separated from their weaving in the web you'll have to pull it apart without destroying the web. It's not so easy.

H: Does the victim who committed these acts realize that he was taken over?

E: I do not believe he would know this. No.

H: Is there anything in his unconscious that might be brought out to help us?

E: Under hypnosis you may strike the note.

H: What about the victims? Are they still in the house or have they gone on? I mean the recent victims.

E: They sometimes do come and wander, and sob.

H: Are they aware of what really happened?

E: Those who do return here are not entirely on the other side. But we are taking note of this and *we will release them from the house.*

H: Do they blame the one that killed them in any way or are they aware of the circumstances?

E: They are not yet aware of the circumstances because they are not yet on the other side completely. Violence sometimes takes a long time before the entrance into the other dimension instead of just being in limbo.

H: Can we help them understand the circumstances?

E: Well, we're taking care of that. You can't get to it.

H: Is there anything else that needs to be done here?

E: That is the root of all the evil – we have to dig it up with various individuals.

H: To your knowledge, was one individual taken over or was more than one taken over here? I mean during that recent situation.

E: It seems that there could be a second one, but not like the first.

H: Who is the second one that might also be involved?

E: It is a younger man.

H: A younger person, male or female?

E: Male.

H: Were any females involved?

E: Yes. I meant to say the younger one was but that's hard when you see it sometimes, it's hard to see whether it's male or female.

H: There were two people involved, altogether, who were taken over?

E: Yes.

H: One male and one female?

E: Yes.

H: Both . . . of what age?

E: Mature, but youngish – not old or decrepit.

H: All right now, is there anything else that we have missed in this account that you can give us?

E: That is the basic . . . if we handle this it will be to bring to you the victim or victims when they did not have to come into this house.

H: Are they free to go elsewhere if we should make contact with them?

E: We can bring them.

H: All right then, would you eventually arrange for such a session with them?

E: I will do so.

H: In the meantime would you please help them to free themselves from this house.

E: That is the reason we are here today.

H: All right. Thank you very much. Then bring the instrument back to herself.

E: I feel like somebody has choked me. Albert is saying that one of the individuals will take over. Now that we have given them their freedom they would like to talk, but otherwise than in *this* environment.

H: I understand. I will make an arrangement to speak to them outside this environment.

E: Albert will ask them if another room is better.

H: Another room? Downstairs? Upstairs? Do you mean other than this room. The house is all right but in another room? Is that correct?

E: No, I was just wondering if there was another room that was a little quieter

H: All right, we will look for one.

H: Here – what do you hear in here?

E: Screaming.

H: Who's screaming?

E: I don't see right now. I'm just hearing.

H: This is one of the rooms on the second floor. (pause) What did Albert say?

E: *Four people have been killed here. A family.*

H: How were they killed?

E: *I hear pistol shots.*

H: Who is doing the killing?

E: *There is one of the younger men.*

H: *Is he doing the killing under the influence of someone else?*

E: *Yes, yes, yes.*

H: Who is the other person?

E: That's the one with the underslung jaw. They think he's crazy – the one who did it.

H: But he's not crazy?

E: *No, he was taken over.*

H: What else did they make him do?

E: Oh, cut up everything that's nasty. Terrible.

H: *Did he do all the killing himself?*

E: *Yes.*

H: Did anybody else do any of the killings or was it all him?

E: All him. Under the influence of this – *absolutely under the influence of a ghost.*

H: Is he innocent then?

E: In his right mind he is innocent. They think he's crazy. I don't think he's quite free either, yet.

H: You mean they can still get to him if he were in this house?

E: I think so. Yes.

H: The ones he killed are free from this house?

E: They are wandering around. They come here and they scream and go. I've been hearing screaming here all the time – so that they can't talk.

H: Is Albert going to help them?

E: Yes he said.

H: Is there anything else that we should know that would give us proof that this was under the influence of the Indian?

E: It's a difficult thing. However, they are so upset about it. As he said before, who is going to believe – who is going to believe? And he's almost in tears about it.

H: Is there any incident that happened to this person before the crime took place that would show he was taken over before?

E: *There was irregular behavior.*

H: What did he do that was irregular.

E: *Fall into violent temper at times.*

H: Did he do anything that was contrary to his normal character?

E: I would say so he says.

H: What sort of things?

E: Cutting up things – and he might have taken it out on pets.

H: Now people who have lived here before – prior to

this particular group of people – did they express anything of this kind?

E: Not so much. They did, but it was not so much because there wasn't a catalyst that was as good as this individual was.

H: And what about the people who came in here afterwards? Recently. Did they experience anything?

E: I would say that they must have felt the depression and heard screams and sounds.

H: Would anybody moving in here still feel the same things?

E: Yes, if they were a catalyst, yes. It would be a depressive house under all circumstances. Terribly depressive. Unless the Indians are put to rest, and that's what Albert wants to do – to save the house.

H: All right. That we can do elsewhere. Or do we do this here?

E: No, it can be done elsewhere.

H: All right. Then ask Albert to protect this house in the meantime to free the ones who were murdered here and we will meet again.

5

The Investigation Continues

As I became more familiar with the bizarre aspects of the DeFeo case, and wondered whether in fact Ethel Meyers was right in suggesting possession as being heavily involved, I attempted to find in the trial records anything that might hint at such an explanation. In this I became convinced that DeFeo himself might not realize what was taking place, or whether he might be acting on the alien influences. Thus I thought it best to look through the account of the trial itself for any clues which ordinary jurists might see in one light while I, as a trained psychic researcher, would evaluate somewhat differently, or perhaps in addition to what appeared to be the obvious explanation and possibly offer a secondary explanation.

Ronald DeFeo, Jr, had a girlfriend by the name of Mindy Weiss, who worked at a local pub. There were elements in her testimony I found of use in pursuing my line of reasoning, as to whether Ronald DeFeo was in fact under influences of a paranormal nature.

* * *

Riverhead, New York
October 29, 1975

MINDY WEISS, Massapequa Park, New York, called as a witness in behalf of the Defendant, having been first duly sworn, testified as follows:

DIRECT EXAMINATION BY MR WEBER:

* * *

Q: Mindy, at about June of 1974, were you living at home?

A: No.

Q: Did you have an apartment then?

A: Yes, I did.

Q: Do you recall an incident that occurred while you were working at Longfellow's and Ronnie came into the bar?

A: Ronnie came in – I don't remember who was with him – and he ordered a drink, and I served him. And he tasted it and he accused me of poisoning him, and he buckled over on the side and said someone poisoned him.

Q: Had you on occasion had opportunity to observe people who were in an intoxicated condition?

A: Yes.

Q: In your opinion was he in an intoxicated condition at that time?

A: No, sir.

Q: Now, will you describe what you observed Ronnie to do at the time he accused you of poisoning him?

A: He buckled over on the bar as if he had, like, a pain.

Q: Now, in your opinion were those acts that you observed at that time, were they irrational or rational acts.

A: Completely irrational.

Q: Mindy, do you recall an incident that occurred at your apartment late one evening during the summer months?

A: Yes. He came with maybe four or five friends over to my apartment.

Q: What happened on that occasion?

A: They came in, and everything was all right. And then very suddenly, Ronnie started a fight. With all of them.

Q: In your opinion was Ronnie in an intoxicated condition at that time?

A: No, sir.

Q: What, if anything, did you observe his friends trying to do?

A: I observed Ronnie egging them on to fight. And they said to Ronnie, 'What's the matter with you?' They tried to calm him down.

Q: Mindy, what, if anything did you do at that point?

A: I interfered to try and calm Ronnie down. And he was in a violent mood, and he pushed me, shoved me across the floor, at which point I went to my bedroom and I snuck out of my window and I went to my parents' house.

Q: Before that occurred, had you observed Ronald do anything with any objects in your house?

A: He picked up a chair and threw it through the ceiling.

Q: Now, Mindy, at the time you observed these acts, in your opinion were they rational or irrational acts?

A: Totally irrational. Irrational.

Q: Mindy, you mentioned to us that you had dinner on occasion at Ronnie's house? Was this in the presence of other members of his family?

A: Yes.

Q: On these occasions will you describe Ronnie's conduct with his family during dinner?

A: He was rational, he was quiet.

Q: Did he ever discuss with you his feelings towards his brothers and sisters?

A: He told me that he loved them and there isn't anything he wouldn't give them if he could.

Q: Mindy, since Ronnie was arrested for this, have you visited him at the Suffolk County Jail?

A: Yes, sir.

Q: Now, Mindy, do you recall what Ronnie said to you on September 26th when you went to see him at the Suffolk County Jail?

A: Well, he said, 'What are you doing here?' And most of his statements were rambling.

Q: Mindy, can you recall what Ronnie told you on September 26th in the Suffolk County Jail?

A: He asked me why I thought his parents and brothers and sisters were dead; that they were killed in self-defense, something like that.

Q: Do you recall any conversations with Ronnie concerning his wanting to leave his home?

A: Yes. He wanted to move out of his house on numerous occasions, but he never did.

Q: Do you recall an occasion where Ronnie came to your apartment one night and wanted you to go out with him.

A: Yes.

Q: Would you describe what happened then? Well, first can we get the approximate time?

A: September again, '74. He came to my house, and to the best of my recollection, it was late. He wanted to go out and I didn't want to go. So he took my car keys and I chased him out of the house and he got in the car. So I got in the car with him. He was behind the driving wheel and he was speeding up and down Merrick Road like a wild man. I got out of the car when he stopped. Then I went to his home to get his father after him to calm him down. And it was late. I remember, I woke them up. His father came out and took me with him in the car to the bar where he was. It was in front of the Chatter Box bar on Merrick Road. When he saw his father he got very angry, and he pushed me on the ground. Then his father grabbed him and said, 'Apologize to the girl.' Grabbed him, physically grabbed him.

Q: Did Ronnie strike his father at that point?

A: No. Ronnie's father grabbed him telling him to apologize to me. And then Ronnie managed to break from his grip and just ran away.

Q: Were there any occasions, Mindy, where Ronnie visited with members of your family?

A: Around September '74, Ronnie came to dinner with my family.

Q: Will you describe Ronnie's conduct at that time?

A: Perfect gentleman. Quiet, reserved, polite.

CROSS-EXAMINATION OF MINDY WEISS, BY MR SULLIVAN:

Q: Okay. Do you recall an incident of a gentleman coming up to you in the Intrepid on one occasion and complimenting you about your body, your figure?

A: I have been complimented before.

Q: Miss Weiss, do you recall an incident where after such compliment you exposed your breasts to this individual?

A: I resent that absolutely.

MR WEBER: Unless the District Attorney has the name of that person who is willing to testify in this courtroom, I ask that that be stricken from the record, the jury admonished not to even consider it, and that the District Attorney be reprimanded for bringing such a question up.

Mr Sullivan: I'm prepared to call a witness on the subject, Judge. He'll be here in just a moment.

The Court: We will wait.

Mr Weber: Your Honor, before the witness is called, may I have that specific question read back?

The Court: Yes, would you read it back, Mr Rowe?

(Whereupon the following was read back by the Reporter: 'Question. Miss Weiss, do you recall an incident where after such a compliment you exposed your breasts to this individual?')

Mr Weber: I want to know if this witness was an eyewitness or is it a hearsay witness?

The Court: We will find all this out when the witness is called.

Mr Sullivan: I call Detective George Harrison.

Mr Weber: If the witness wishes to leave, she may. I'm not requesting that she leave.

The Court: Would you prefer to leave, Miss Weiss?

The Witness: No. I'd like to hear this.

Detective George Harrison, called as a witness in behalf of the people, having been previously duly sworn, resumed the stand, and testified further as follows:

Direct Examination by Mr Sullivan:

Q: Within the recent four or five weeks did you, at my request, reopen certain aspects of the investigation in relation to this case?

A: I did, sir.

Q: And did those aspects of the investigation take you back into certain areas of Massapequa and Amityville?

A: Yes, sir.

Q: And have you talked to certain persons who frequented and patronized bars and drinking establishments there?

A: I did.

Q: Did some of those conversations relate to Mindy Weiss?

A: Yes, sir, they did.

Q: Did there come a time when you discussed a specific act that Mindy Weiss engaged in with one or more of the people that you have named?

A: I can only comment on one act. I hesitate to state it. If it took place at the Intrepid, if that's what you are talking about, sir.

Q: All right. Proceed to tell us what you were told.

A: And if I may, is this the act in which she revealed herself that we are talking about?

Q: That's what I'm asking you about, Detective Harrison.

A: Yes, sir. Someone commented to Miss Weiss in the terms that were related to me – I'll repeat them almost exactly – 'You have a nice pair of tits.' At that point Miss Weiss revealed them.

THE COURT: Bring the jury in.

(The jury entered the jury box at 4:09 p.m.)

THE CLERK: Jury is all present.

THE COURT: Mr Rowe, would you read to the witness the last question that was put to her before the jury retired?

(Whereupon the following was read back by the Reporter: 'Question. Miss Weiss, do you recall an incident where after such a compliment you exposed your breasts to this individual?')

THE COURT: You may answer, Miss.

A: No. Absolutely not. And I still resent the question.

FRANCIS DAVIDGE, Amityville, New York, called as a witness in behalf of the Defendant, having been first duly sworn, testified as follows:

DIRECT EXAMINATION BY MR WEBER:

Q: Mr Davidge, how old are you, sir?

A: Twenty-four.

Q: Frank, I take you to an incident that occurred the summertime of 1972 when you were on a double date with Ronnie DeFeo. Do you recall that?

A: Yes, I do.

Q: Will you tell the Court and jury what happened at that time?

A: Ronnie and I had been on a double date. We had gone to the movies and when we were done we got something to eat at a diner. We had dropped my date off and we drove to Ronnie's house in his car and we dropped his date off. And the girl got out of the car and Ronnie got out of the car and closed the door. I guess they were going to say good night or something. And I was sitting in the back seat. And maybe a minute or two passed by and Ronnie yanked open the car door, and under the front seat of the car he had a rifle. And he took the rifle out of the car and ran outside of the car with it. And I jumped out of the car and I saw him. Over the trunk of the car he had the girl bent over the trunk, and he had the rifle pointed at her head and he was yelling something at her. He was verbally threatening her. I can't recall exactly what he said. I took the gun out of his hands. I yanked it out of his hands. I threw the gun on the back seat of the car and I took Ronnie by the arm and I said, 'Let's go. We have to leave.' And I literally threw Ronnie into the car, and we drove away.

Q: Frank, would you describe those acts and conduct that you saw as rational or irrational?

A: I would say it was irrational.

Q: Frank, I recall your attention to November of 1972, when you were on a hunting trip with Ronnie DeFeo and others.

A: Ronnie DeFeo, myself and two of our friends had gone on a hunting trip upstate, and we decided that we would go into the woods grouped in pairs of twos, and that the two other friends had gone together and that Ronnie and I would go together. And I drew a diagram on the ground with a stick with Ronnie, and I said that we would walk through the woods together and that I would be to his extreme right and he would be to my left; and that if we had seen anything walking to the deer path that his right and my left would be totally out of firing range, there would be no shooting in that direction. We had gotten in there about a half a mile maybe into the woods and Ronnie was starting to get too far in front of me. I said, 'Hey, Ron, slow down.' And he didn't answer me. I just passed a tree and I walked past the tree and I saw him there. He was looking in my direction and he had the gun pointing directly at me. I stepped back about two feet and I was behind a tree and I heard three shots. And one of the shots had gone by me so close that I could see the branches of the tree falling down. And the shots were evenly spaced about two or three seconds apart. And after the shots were over, I waited a moment, and then I was scared, I was mad, and I peered out from behind the tree and I saw Ronnie in the same place that he was before he fired the shots. He had the gun pointed at the ground and he was looking at the ground. I started to run up to him screaming, 'What's the matter with you? Don't you remember the diagram? Why did you shoot in my direction?' While I was walking up to him he did nothing but look at the ground and hold the gun pointing at the ground. Then when I approached him, I put the questions upon him again, and he looked at the ground for another ten seconds. Then he looked up at me and he said, 'What's the matter, Remus? Why are you so excited? Relax.' I was screaming and I put the same questions to him again, and he said the same thing again. And then he said, 'Let's go on. Let's keep hunting. Let's go into the woods.' At that point I didn't want to go into the woods with him, and I turned around and left.

Q: Frank, would you describe those acts that afternoon as rational or irrational?

A: I would say it was irrational.

And finally, it was the accused's turn to be questioned.

(Nov. 5., 1975.) (Jury seated at 2:10 p.m.)

THE CLERK: Jury is all present.

THE COURT: All right, you may proceed, Mr Weber.

MR WEBER: Thank you very much, your Honor. Defense calls Ronald DeFeo, Jr, your Honor.

RONALD JOSEPH DEFEO, JR, residing at Suffolk County Jail, New York, called as a witness in his own behalf, being first duly sworn, testified as follows:

DIRECT EXAMINATION BY MR WEBER:

Q: Did you hear Detective Gozaloff state that you told him that you and Kelske had burned your father's boat to collect the insurance proceeds?

A: Yes, sir, I heard him say that.

Q: Did you ever burn any boat, Ronnie?

A: No, sir. In fact, my boat, it should be in the water, Boatland in Lindenhurst, where I left it before this incident happened.

Q: Did you hear Detective Gozaloff testify that you said you robbed the house next door to you?

A: I never even knew the house next door was robbed.

Q: When for the first time did you consider yourself a suspect in this case, Ronnie?

A: When they took a paraffin test on my hands. That's about nine o'clock in the First Precinct. And they started asking me questions about guns.

Q: Did you know you were guilty at that time?

A: I'm not sure, I don't think so.

Q: Do you know if you are guilty today?

A: No, I am not guilty of what these people are charging me with.

Q: Do you remember any particular incident that occurred, Ronnie, that caused your parents to take you to the psychiatrist?

A: Well, I was in my house in Amityville, and my mother and father went out, and my grandfather and grandmother, Mr Brigante and Mrs Brigante, came out from Brooklyn, and they were baby-sitting at the house for myself and the kids.

And me and my grandfather, I don't know what he did, he did something, and I never did it to him before, but I called him a fuck. And he took his belt off and he was going to try to hit me with it.

I picked up a lamp, something, and started throwing things at him, throwing chairs, threw everything at him, a lot of stuff. He chased me through the house, I ran up the stairs, and somehow I banged into my sister Dawn.

I don't know why I did it, but I started beating her brains out, I just started punching her and I couldn't stop. He pulled me off her. Right after that, the incident, they took me to a psychiatrist.

Q: And how long did you continue going to this psychiatrist, Ronnie?

A: About a year and a half.

Q: Well, Ronnie, when you were 15 and going to St Francis Prep, there was yelling and screaming at your house, you say?

A: Yes, sir, there was yelling and screaming and fighting since I can remember – 13, 12. It's been like that right up till this incident.

Q: What did you do about the yelling and screaming?

A: Well, I tried to run away. And every time I ran away I got brought back.

Q: How were the conditions at home when you were going to Amityville?

A: They were very very bad. That's when I started to use drugs. I couldn't take living in my house, and I felt if I had to live in my house I had to do something about it. So, to take my mind off it, I used drugs.

Q: Ronnie, while you were going to Amityville High School, did you ever have any money problems?

A: I never had any money problems.

Q: Could you explain what you mean?

A: Well, my mother and father gave me all the money I wanted. They gave me everything I wanted. I wanted a car, a boat, whatever I wanted. I always had it all.

Q: Do you remember you telling me about your notice, your draft notice?

A: Yes, sir.

Q: What did the psychiatrist tell you, Ronnie?

A: I better put myself in a mental institution before I wind up killing someone. That's exactly what he said.

Q: Did you tell this to anybody?

A: Yes, sir, I told it to Mr Diorio, I told it to my father, I told it to my mother, I told it to my brothers and sisters, I told it to all of my relatives.

Q: Do you recall an incident during this time when you went to see a movie, and as a result of that you did something when you got out of it.

A: Yes, sir, That's the night I smacked my car up.

Q: Was there a particular scene in the movie that . . .

A: Yes, sir, the movie was about a man that drove a car, and at the end of the picture he wound up killing himself. And when I got out of the movie, I don't know what happened, we were coming down the Southern State Parkway. I didn't see nobody on the road. I had it down to the floor. I was running a hundred, 110 miles an hour with Rod Hicks in the car. And I just kept going. He told me to stop. I told him to shut up. We started arguing. I just kept going. I saw the traffic up ahead, but my foot wouldn't come off the gas pedal. It was like somebody nailed to the gas pedal. I couldn't stop. He pulled the keys out of the ignition, slammed on the brakes, and took the wheel out of my hand. Maybe a quarter of a mile before we got up to them cars I was going right into the back of them. I was going to hit somebody right in the rear. The car went over the divider into the woods, tore two or three trees down. It ripped the whole back of my car off. After we hit the divider and all, I didn't know what happened. He had to tell me.

Q: Now, up to the point that you had seen the psychiatrist, did you make any efforts to get out of your house?

A: Yes, sir; I made a lot of efforts. I could not take no more in that house, and I went and saw a specific girl, this was before Miss Weiss. I believe her name was Karen. I told her of the problem I was having. 'Listen, I got to get out of my house. You got to do me a favor. Tell my mother and father you are pregnant and I got to marry you.' And she told them that. And I left the house that night and went with her back to her house. I was going to live at her apartment. A couple of hours later my father had found out where she lived. He came over there and gave the girl a thousand dollars and told her to get an abortion and dragged me out of the house.

Q: Were there any other occasions that you left your house?

A: Before this happened, yes, sir. It was not Mindy Weiss. It was some other girl. I think her name was Jackie.

Q: What happened on that occasion?

A: Well, I told everybody in my house, every one of them, I was going to kill them, I got to get out of here. I said, 'I'm going to kill you if I stay here.' I kept telling them.

Q: Will you tell us what happened with this girl Jackie?

A: I moved in with her. And I don't remember if it was the first day or the second day – I woke up one morning and came out of her apartment to get in my car, and my car was gone. But before I called the police I took her car and I went to my house with her. When I got to my house, my car was in the driveway. All the spark plug wires and the coil wire were gone. I called my father up and I told him, 'Listen, I'm tired of this.' I said, 'You took my car.' He said, 'I'll give you your car back.' He said, 'I don't care if you come to work or not. I'll give you all the money you want. All I want you to do is live in this house.' I told him, 'I can't come back there and live with you.' All he said, 'No, no, you got to come back here. Don't worry about it.' He thought it was a big joke. I went back there and lived.

THE COURT: When exactly did you take these threats to your family?

THE WITNESS: I think that was in July or August.

Mr Weber: I object to Your Honor's characterizing them as threats. They could also be warnings.

Q: When you told them this, Ronnie, did you still love them?

A: Yes, sir. I didn't want to kill them. To be quite honest about it, it's not that I wanted to do it, I had no choice. I had to do it.

Q: During the summer of 1974, Ronnie, were you having any other problems other than what you have already described?

A: Yes, sir. There was a lot. One of them was women. I had a lot of girl friends and I had a lot of sex with the girls I went out with. I wasn't a sex maniac or anything. All of a sudden, women seemed to be turning me off. I thought it might have been a specific girl, but it wasn't a specific girl. It was all women. They just completely turned me off. I had nothing but trouble.

Q: When did this happen?

A: This was all in the period of time right before the killings, a couple of months, all this started happening.

Q: Did you do anything about that? Did you go to see a doctor?

A: I never went to see a doctor. I was going to go see a doctor, but I never did.

Q: How was your hearing at that time?

Mr Sullivan: I object.

The Court: You claim that his ability to hear is relevant?

Mr Weber: No, *what* he was hearing is relevant.

A: I was hearing voices. I heard voiccs all the time.

Q: Ronnie, what do you recall happening the night of November 13th?

A: I blacked out or fell asleep. Somebody came down there and started kicking me. And when I got up the TV was off, the lamp was off, the room was pretty dark. All I know is somebody was standing there with a rifle in their hands and the hands that the person had were black.

Q: Ronnie, who was the person?

A: I thought it was my sister, Dawn. That's who I thought it was, to be quite honest about it. And I remember there was some conversation about this here, and she said she was going to kill everybody.

I remember taking the rifle away from her. And when I took the rifle away from her, I don't remember where I went exactly, back in the sitting room or out in the hallway, she seemed to disappear. I remember taking the rifle from there and going to my mother and father's room with it.

I walked in the door. I didn't go that far in the door, a couple of feet, maybe. And I just started to shoot. I don't know if it was three times or four times, but I started to shoot the gun, fire the gun.

Q: Ronnie, as you were shooting the gun, did you hear the noise of the rifle?

A: No, sir, that gun didn't make any noise. There was no noise in the house. There were no lights on at that time, as far as I remember. The only light that was on was the bathroom next to Allison's room, they left that light on in that bathroom. That was the only light I remember being on on that floor.

And after I shot my mother and father, I put the gun down and left it on the floor. I went back in the sitting room. I sat down on the chair. I was sitting in the sitting room, and the next thing I heard, it didn't sound like it was close, it sounded like it was real far away. I heard shots going on, gun shots. And when I did get up to look, I could have sworn it was my sister that came out of that room and ran up the stairs with a rifle in her hand.

Q: What did you do then, Ronnie?

A: Well, this whole time I was very very calm, through all of this. I wasn't mad, I was completely calm. I walked up the stairs. And when I got up there I believed that I saw Dawn loading the rifle.

I remember seeing her loading the rifle. And I remember fighting with her. I know I wanted to throw her out of the window of her bedroom. That was on the third floor, it was pretty high. I was going to throw her out the window, but I didn't throw her out the window.

I remember pushing her down onto her bed and, somehow, I don't remember what point of time I got the gun, but I remember pushing her down. And I shot her.

After that, I heard footsteps. When I came out of the room, I could have sworn I saw somebody else running down the stairs. So I ran down the stairs. When I got down to the first floor, the front door was open. And I went out the front door. I might have been on the stoop and went as far as the driveway in the front of my house. I saw somebody or something running across the Ireland's front lawn. That's what I believe did happen in that house. Whether or not it's my imagination or my mind is playing tricks on me, I don't know.

Q: What did you do after that?

A: Well, after that I went back in the house. I closed the door. I went back upstairs. I don't remember what I did first or what had happened. I know I took a shower. But I think the first thing I did was I cleaned the place up. The place was a mess. There was garbage all over the place. I was going to take everything and put everything in a big pile, just leave it there.

I know now that my family was dead and I felt good about it, I felt very good. Because the threat to my life was over with, it was no longer a danger. I had to start worrying about my relatives. I had plans to kill all them, too.

Q: And then what did you do?

A: Eventually I left. I didn't know at that time whether or not I should call the police, because I felt if I did call the police at that time I would have been arrested, you know, for this. And I felt that it was my obligation, my job to bury them.

And so I didn't try to hide nothing. In fact, I'm the one that told the police where everything was. And I put everything where I knew that I can get at it again when the time did come for me to turn myself in and to tell the police what had happened.

* * *

Up to now, I have presented excerpts and references from both the pre-trial examination and the trial itself; I am sure very few of my audience have ever actually been at a trial such as this, where the life of the defendant is at stake. I thought it useful, therefore to present an actual, uncensored, uncut and unedited version of every word and motion made at the trial, to show the intricacies and manoeuvers occurring in a Court of Law under these circumstances.

Grace Fagan is a young lady who befriended the late

Dawn DeFeo, and also knew the defendant and the entire family for many years. John Carswell is a friend of Ronnie's, and also in a good position to fill in many sidelights pertaining to Ronnie's personal life and to those strange actions that had rapidly become the focal point of the proceedings.

Herewith are the minutes of what transpired in Court:

Riverhead, New York
October 30, 1975

(EXCERPT FROM DIRECT EXAMINATION OF THE WITNESS GRACE FAGAN·)

GRACE FAGAN, Prospect Street, Amityville, New York, called as a witness in behalf of the Defendant, having been first duly sworn, testified as follows:

DIRECT EXAMINATION BY MR WEBER:

* * *

Q: And were you a classmate of Dawn DeFeo?

A: Yes, I was.

Q: Will you describe your relationship with Dawn DeFeo?

A: She was my girl friend.

Q: Did you know Mrs Louise DeFeo?

A: Yes, I did.

Q: And Mr Ronnie DeFeo, Sr?

A: Yes.

Q: Butch, or Ronnie DeFeo, Jr, did you know him?

A: Yes.

Q: How long have you known the DeFeo family?

A: Three years.

Q: Did you spend much time at their home?

A: Yes, I did.

Q: Will you tell us approximately how much time you spent at their home?

A: Seven days a week.

Q: Did you have opportunities to observe Butch in his relationship with his family?

A: Yes.

Q: Will you describe Butch's relationship with his brothers, Grace?

A: He was very close to all the kids in the family.

Q: And is that the same for his sisters?

A: Yes.

Q: Will you describe Butch's relationship with his mother?

A: He was close to his mother.

MR SULLIVAN: I'm going to object. That's a conclusion, Judge.

THE COURT: All right, Miss Fagan, you can tell us what you saw or what you might have heard.

THE WITNESS: He seemed close to his mother.

MR SULLIVAN: I object on the same ground.

THE COURT: You can't give us your conclusion. Do you understand what I'm talking about, Miss Fagan?

THE WITNESS: No.

THE COURT: You can tell us anything you saw occur between the Defendant and any of his family or anything you heard said between them, but not your mental conclusion. Do you understand, Miss?

THE WITNESS: Yes.

Q: Now, with the Judge's instructions, Grace, can you describe for us Butch's relationship with his mother?

A: He got along with his mother.

Q: Did you have opportunity or occasions to observe Butch around the house?

A: Yes.

Q: Did you observe him doing any work at the house on occasion?

MR SULLIVAN: I object, Judge. That's irrelevant.

THE COURT: No, I'll allow it.

A: Yes, I did.

Q: What did you observe?

A: Well, he put the statues on the front lawn – he put them all together with his friend – and he put the fountain that was on the front.

Q: I can't hear you.

THE COURT: Can you hear the witness? Speak up, Miss Fagan, a little louder.

A: He did, like, a lot of housework around the house. He did painting. Like, he put the statues up and raked leaves, cleaned the pool. Just general housework.

Q: Grace, I call your attention to the summer of 1974. Was there an occasion when you were riding in a car with Butch and Dawn?

A: Yes.

Q: Do you recall that occasion?

A: Yes.

Q: Was there a discussion about the Amityville Police at that time?

A: Yes, there was.

Q: Will you tell us how the discussion came about and who said what as you were riding in the car?

A: We were driving down Broadway, and as we were driving down there was an Amityville cop going the other way, and he just looked at us. So Butch said, 'See, he knows you, too.' And he said that we better watch out because he knows us and to watch our step.

Q: Now, at the time Butch said that to you, did you consider those words rational or irrational?

MR SULLIVAN: I'm going to object. There is no foundation for an opinion as to rationality on an incident or an event like that.

MR WEBER: Well, your Honor, maybe we should leave that up to the psychiatrist. With the Court's permission, I would ask the witness be allowed to answer, and the psychiatrist will connect it.

THE COURT: All right, I'll allow the witness to answer. Go ahead, Miss.

A: Could you repeat the question?

Q: Did you consider those words coming from Butch rational or irrational?

A: Irrational, at the time.

Q: Now, Grace, I call your attention to September or October of 1974. Were you at the DeFeo residence and did you have a conversation with Butch in the presence of Dawn DeFeo?

A: I don't know what you mean.

Q: All right. Were you and Dawn DeFeo preparing to go out some place?

A: Oh, yes.

Q: And did you have a conversation with Butch at that time?

A: Yes.

Q: What did Butch tell you?

A: He told us that – not to hang around where he hung around; and if we ever saw, like, his car where we were going, not to go in because we would just get in trouble because they probably wouldn't let us in because they didn't like him.

Q: Did he say who the 'they' were?

A: No.

Q: Now, at the time Butch told you this, did you consider those words rational or irrational?

MR SULLIVAN: Judge, I'm going to object. An event

such as this cannot support or form the basis for an opinion as to rationality.

THE COURT: No, I'm going to allow the witness to describe how she considered this remark. Go ahead, Miss.

A: I'd say irrational.

Q: Grace, I call your attention to September 26, 1974. Did that date have any particular significance to you?

A: It was the day Mark got hurt.

Q: Do you recall the date of Butch's birthday?

A: Oh, yes.

Q: Were you at Butch's house on that day?

A: Yes, I was.

Q: Will you describe what, if anything, occurred on September 26, 1974?

A: We had a cake for him because it was his birthday. And—

Q: Who was present?

A: Besides me, just the family. His mother, his father, and the kids, and him. That's it. And we had a cake for him and we had his presents and all.

MR SULLIVAN: I can't hear the witness.

THE COURT: Miss Fagan, again would you try to speak up a lot louder? You may continue.

A: (Continuing) Well, he blew out the candles on this cake and he opened his presents and all; then he went around and kissed everybody, thanking them.

Q: Each member of his family?

A: Yes.

Q: Do you recall an incident during the summer of 1974—

MR SULLIVAN: Now, Judge, I'm going to object to that. That has no relationship to any fact in issue on this case.

MR WEBER: Which one, my question or the answer?

THE COURT: Does his conduct at the birthday have anything to do with any issue in this case?

MR WEBER: Yes, it does, your Honor.

THE COURT: In what way?

MR WEBER: Your Honor, these things are going to be connected up by the psychiatrist.

THE COURT: His conduct at the birthday party just testified to?

MR WEBER: That's correct.

THE COURT: All right. Go ahead.

Q: Do you recall an incident during the summer of 1974, Grace, when you were at the DeFeo house seated at the table with the young DeFeo boys, Mark and John, when Butch walked into the kitchen?

A: Yes.

Q: Did Butch say something in your presence to his brothers?

A: It was me and Dawn and the three kids were all there. And I'm not sure, one of them said something . . . I'm not sure exactly what they said . . . but he said . . .

Q: Who is the 'he'?

A: Butch. He told them not to look up to him, that to look up to Dawn because Dawn was going to school and

Dawn was going to make it in this world, and not to take after his example.

Q: Grace, were you ever in Butch's presence—

MR SULLIVAN: I'm going to object and move to strike it, Judge. These have no relationship to any fact in issue. And I'm willing to be shown how this could form or support the basis for any admissible opinion by a psychiatrist. We might as well go into any fact or event or anything that ever happened in the Defendant's life if this sort of material is going to be admitted.

MR WEBER: I'm willing to do that, your Honor.

THE COURT: What relevancy does this alleged remark to his brothers have?

MR WEBER: Your Honor, the Defendant's relationship to his family in the few months prior to this incident I think has the most vital relationship to this case.

THE COURT: All right, I'm allowing this on the strength of your statement to me that this is going to be related to opinion evidence in this case.

MR WEBER: Thank you, your Honor.

THE COURT: All right, go ahead.

Q: Grace, were you in the company of Butch on occasions when he discussed other people? Yes or no.

A: I don't know what you mean.

Q: Do you recall being in Butch's presence during the summer of 1974 when a conversation took place concerning what he thought of what other people thought about him?

MR SULLIVAN: Object. I object to the form of the question.

THE COURT: It is much too broad.

MR WEBER: Your Honor, I don't want to put the words in the witness' mouth.

THE COURT: All right. Do you wish to confer with your witness privately?

MR WEBER: If I may, your Honor.

THE COURT: You may.

MR WEBER: Grace, can I see you for a minute?

THE COURT: Step down, Miss Fagan. (Whereupon Mr Weber and the witness conferred privately.)

MR WEBER: Thank you, your Honor. (Whereupon the witness resumed the stand.)

Q: Grace, do you recall another conversation you had with Butch during the summer of 1974 concerning what he said about other people?

A: He said that he had a lot of enemies and a lot of people didn't like him, that a lot of people would like to see him dead.

Q: Can you recall approximately how many times Butch had mentioned this to you?

A: Not that many. Once or twice maybe.

Q: Now, did you know, Grace, that Butch was on probation—

A: yes.

Q: —the year prior to this, the death of his family?

A: Yes, I did.

Q: Now, prior to that year that he was on probation, did you have occasions to be in his car?

A: Yes, I did.

Q: And did you ever find anything in his car?

A: Well, we didn't find anything in his car; we found it in his father's car which he used sometimes.

Q: What did you find?

A: We found the cap of a needle; that's all we found in the car. We found different things in other places.

Q: When did you find these?

A: When?

Q: Yes. Was it a year before this, the death of his family?

A: It was before he was on probation. It was about a year.

THE COURT: We have already heard proof in this case that the date of sentence of probation was some day in December, 1973. So you are now questioning her as to events prior to that time?

MR WEBER: Prior, yes.

THE COURT: All right.

Q: Now, after December of '73 while Butch was on probation did you have occasions to be in his car or his father's car?

A: Yes.

Q: Did you have occasions to be in the bedroom?

A: Yes.

Q: Did you have occasions to be in the other bedrooms in the house?

A: Yes.

Q: Did you ever find any paraphernalia used for narcotic purposes or drugs?

A: After he was on probation?

Q: Yes.

A: No.

Q: Grace, were you at the DeFeo residence on November 9th, which was a Saturday, of 1974?

A: Yes.

Q: Will you describe – About what time were you there?

A: I was there most of the day.

Q: Did you see Butch at that time?

A: Yes.

Q: Will you tell us where you saw him?

A: I saw him in the house first.

Q: All right. And then what, if anything, did you see him do?

A: Well, his father told us to – all of us, me and Dawn and him – he told us to go out and start raking the leaves up outside. So we all went out. The three of us went outside and we started, me and Dawn, putting them all in a pile, and he lit them. So Dawn told him he shouldn't have done it because his father was going to get mad. With that, her father came out and he started yelling because he lit them on fire.

Q: Did his father have anything in his hand?

A: He picked up a shovel.

Q: What, if anything, did you observe him do with the shovel?

A: He started yelling. He started swinging it at him, toward him.

Q: At who?

A: At Butch.

Q: What, if anything, did Butch do?

A: He didn't do anything.

Q: Grace, I call your attention to early September of 1974. Were you at a football game where Mark was injured?

A: Yes.

Q: And later on that afternoon did you have occasion to see Butch at the hospital?

A: We saw him before he went to the hospital.

Q: Then did you see him at the hospital?

A: Yes.

Q: Do you know how Butch got to the hospital?

A: He drove out.

Q: Were you in the car?

A: No.

Q: Where were you?

A: I was in the car with Dawn. We followed him there.

Q: Will you describe the manner in which Butch drove to the hospital?

A: Fast.

Q: And did you see him park his car?

A: No, he got there before us.

Q: When did you see him for the first time at the hospital?

A: Well, we came down the street, we saw him running across the street toward the hospital.

Q: What, if anything, did you see after you saw him running?

A: Well, he got about to the emergency entrance. Just about as he got there his father and his grandfather came out, but I don't know. We were across the street. He apparently wanted to go into the hospital and his father wouldn't let him go in.

Q: What, if anything, did you see his father do?

A: He was holding him back. He wouldn't let him go in.

Q: Did you see Butch strike his father?

A: No, he didn't hit him.

Q: What, if anything, did you see Butch do?

A: He was trying to get away from him.

Q: Grace, in all the occasions that you were ever at the DeFeo house did you ever see Butch strike any member of his family?

MR SULLIVAN: I object. It's irrelevant.

THE COURT: No, I'll allow it.

A: No, I didn't.

MR WEBER: Thank you very much, Grace. No further questions, your Honor.

*   *   *

REDIRECT EXAMINATION BY MR WEBER:

*   *   *

Q: Grace, do you recall telling Mr Sullivan that you didn't recall any incidents where Butch did something without being provoked into doing it? Do you recall saying something to that effect?

A: Yes.

Q: Do you recall an incident where you were walking one of the DeFeo dogs with Mr DeFeo?

A: No.

Q: And Butch – do you recall whether Butch approached with his car? Do you recall that incident?

A: No.

Q: Do you recall Mr Sullivan asking you if Butch ever told you that members of his family were out to get him, and you said no, he never said that?

A: Yes.

Q: Do you recall that? Do you recall instances where Butch indicated to you or told you that other people were out to get him?

A: Yes.

Q: Do you recall those instances?

A: I don't recall the exact incidents. I remember it being said, but I don't remember exactly when.

MR WEBER: Thank you, Grace.

* * *

(EXCERPT FROM DIRECT EXAMINATION OF JOHN A. CARSWELL:)

JOHN A. CARSWELL, Old Sunrise Highway, Massapequa, New York, called as a witness in behalf of the Defendant, having been first duly sworn, testified as follows:

DIRECT EXAMINATION BY MR WEBER:

* * *

Q: Did you have occasions to see Ronnie DeFeo, Jr, on weekends that you were on active duty?

THE COURT: Can we establish at least a time period that we are talking about?

MR WEBER: All right.

Q: Would you give us the time that you were on active duty in upstate New York?

A: Excuse me?

Q: Will you give us the dates that you were on active duty in upstate New York?

A: I was on active duty up to May – up to May, '74.

Q: Prior to that time you have already told us on weekends you would come into Amityville?

A: Right.

Q: Did you have occasions to see Ronnie DeFeo, Jr?

A: We would see each other, run into each other at 'Septembers,' different clubs.

Q: Are you a good friend of Ronnie's?

A: I guess you would say a good friend.

Q: John, have you ever seen Ronnie in the company of any members of his family?

A: Yes, I have.

Q: And do you recall those occasions?

A: Not right offhand, no.

Q: Do you recall any irrational conduct that you may have observed concerning Ronnie and the members of the family?

MR SULLIVAN: I object to the form of the question.

THE COURT: Well, I'm going to allow it. But let's pin it down again to a period at least.

MR WEBER: Your Honor, I don't believe – all right. May the witness answer this question?

THE COURT: This man has said he's known the Defendant since high school days. Let's start pinning this area down.

MR WEBER: After he is finished I think it would be obvious. I'm not going into that particular area.

THE COURT: Then would you put within your question the period that you are talking about, please?

Q: During the period of time that you have known Ronnie, and have seen him in the company of members of his family, have you ever seen Ronnie to act irrationally?

MR SULLIVAN: It is the leading nature of this question that I object to, Judge.

MR WEBER: I withdraw the question.

Q: John, I call your attention to September of 1974. Do you recall an incident that occurred at the Intrepid Bar?

A: Yes, I do.

Q: And where is that bar located?

A: It's located in East Massapequa now. Used to be West Amityville. They rezoned it.

THE COURT: Where was it in September, '74?

THE WITNESS: West Amityville.

Q: Did you see Ronnie DeFeo, Jr, at that time?

A: Yes, I did.

Q: At about what time was it?

A: I would say about 11 o'clock – 11, 12 o'clock in the evening.

Q: What did you observe concerning Ronnie?

A: Well, I just – on that day I just drove into the parking lot, and Ronnie was there already. And he was there with Mindy. And he had, I guess, a revolver or gun in his hand. Definitely it was a gun. And he shot it off in the parking lot. And I went up to him, I said, 'What are you doing?' And I took the thing away from him and I threw it back in his car. Took the clip out of it, threw it under the seat so he couldn't find it, because it was dark. I talked to him for a little while.

Q: Prior to your taking the gun from him, did Ronnie do or say anything to you?

A: Yes, he did. He said, 'I'm going to go inside. I'm going to get him.' That's all he said. I asked him about what. He said, well, they fired Mindy, blah, blah. This carried on about Mindy being fired from there. I said, 'Well, did you talk to the guy yet?' He goes, 'No.' I said, 'Go talk to him.' He did fire the gun off. And he – like he was wild, and he calmed down.

Mr Sullivan: I object and ask it be stricken.

The Court: Mr Carswell, you may solely describe conduct that you observed or language between you and the Defendant and anyone else.

The Witness: All right. Well, we went inside. I talked to the guy. He was calm, and he apologized for what he did out in the parking lot.

Q: The acts and conduct that you observed out in the parking lot, would you describe those acts as being rational or irrational?

A: I'd say irrational.

Q: Had you ever seen Ronnie conduct himself in such a manner prior to that?

Mr Sullivan: I object. Leading.

THE COURT: No, I'll allow that.

A: You mean in an irrational state?

Q: Yes.

A: I would say yes.

Q: Can you tell us where and when you saw him act in a similar manner?

MR SULLIVAN: I object to this leading.

THE COURT: Yes, I'll sustain that as to the form.

Q: Can you tell us when that was, John?

THE COURT: Date, place, and time, please.

A: Well, I was down – I was in 'Septembers.'

Q: That's another bar?

A: Another bar. We used to go down – meet everybody down there. And I met – I ran into Ronnie down there.

MR SULLIVAN: Can we have a date?

THE COURT: Can you also tell the time of the year, the month?

THE WITNESS: It was roughly either the end of October, beginning of November. Sometime in that time.

THE COURT: What year?

THE WITNESS: Last year, '74.

THE COURT: The end of October, beginning of November, 1974. All right.

THE WITNESS: Yes.

A: (Continuing) And I was kidding him about it, what he did down at the 'Intrepid.' And I said, 'Do you remember what you did?' And he goes, 'No, what did I do?' So I explained, and he apologized because he kind of put me on the spot, too. He said, 'I'm sorry.' I said, 'Forget about it.' And he said – he comes up to me and he goes, 'Do you really want to hear something funny?'

MR SULLIVAN: I cannot hear the witness.

Q: Would you please speak louder?

A: He come up to me and said, 'Do you really want to hear something funny?' I said, 'What is it, Ronnie?' He said, 'My father and mother tricked me into going to see a psychiatrist.' I thought he was only—

MR SULLIVAN: I object to the witness' conclusions.

THE COURT: Not what you thought. Mr Carswell, do you understand what I am trying to tell you? You can only testify as to conduct that you saw or words that you heard, not your thoughts.

THE WITNESS: I'm sorry about that.

THE COURT: All right.

A: He said that his mother and father tricked him into seeing a psychiatrist. I said, 'What about it?' He says, well, he talked to him. He talked to his father and his mother. And later on he told him that he was – his father and himself, Ronnie – was dangerous to each other.

MR SULLIVAN: I'm going to object to this. This is rank hearsay. It's multiple hearsay.

THE COURT: You are not permitted, Mr Carswell, to testify as to anything the psychiatrist is supposed to have said. Do you understand?

THE WITNESS: I understand that now.

THE COURT: All right.

Q: What did Ronnie say that he said to the psychiatrist?

MR SULLIVAN: I object to that.

Mr Weber: If anything.

The Court: No, that I'll allow.

A: He said the psychiatrist was nuts.

Mr Weber: Thank you, John.

* * *

Redirect Examination by Mr Weber:

Q: Do you recall telling Mr Sullivan that you never saw Ronnie hit or strike anyone?

A: Right.

Q: Do you recall an incident that occurred at 'Septembers' during September of 1974—

A: Yes, I do.

Q: —wherein someone hit you?

A: Yes.

Mr Sullivan: I object. That's irrelevant.

Mr Weber: Your Honor, I am laying the foundation.

The Court: Is this in the defendant's presence, when you got hit?

The Witness: When I got hit, no.

The Court: All right, then I'll sustain the objection.

THE WITNESS: He was—

THE COURT: I have sustained the objection.

Q: After this incident occurred in 'Septembers' did you see Ronnie?

A: Yes, I did.

Q: How soon after?

A: It was right after it.

Q: Will you tell us what Ronnie did?

A: After that incident happened I left abruptly. And as I left, the owner of the place left, and he said—

MR SULLIVAN: I can't understand the witness.

THE COURT: When he left, the owner of the place left.

A: (Continuing) I left the parking lot abruptly. I just wanted to get out of there. As I left, the owner left right behind me in his car. And he, Ronnie, was sitting down the street, and I pulled over behind him. The owner pulled over. He said, 'Make sure you go to the hospital,' because they had to put stitches above my eye. And Ronnie made sure I went. He was – he told Ronnie, 'Make sure he goes to the hospital.'

Q: Did Ronnie go with you to the hospital?

A: Yes, the Brunswick.

Q: After the hospital, what did Ronnie do?

A: He made sure I went home after that.

Q: Was he involved in that incident?

A: No, he wasn't.

MR SULLIVAN: Judge, I object to this entire redirect as being utterly irrelevant to any issue in this case.

THE COURT: I'll allow it as to the defendant's actions as to the hospital aspect.

MR WEBER: No further questions, your Honor.

* * *

Obviously, different types of investigators would have different views on the case, not only because of their approach but also because of their background and training.

Defense attorney William Weber, a man whose skill and oratory easily rivals the likes of F. Lee Bailey and Marvin Belli, early in the proceedings retained one Herman Race as his private sleuth. Mr Race is a very determined and knowledgeable man: that is, knowledgeable in *his* areas of expertise. These are rather narrowly confined by his long years as a policeman. He is not given to any interest in anything requiring a wider horizon, or subjects which involve the frontiers of the mind. His world is a hard-fact world, in which there would be no room for anything intangible, in the old-fashioned sense. Perhaps old-fashioned *is* the right word for Mr Race. On the hottest day of summer I saw him wear a business suit, complete with tie, and he never once took it off, or complained about the weather.

Here are his statements concerning his activities in respect to the DeFeo case:

R: My name is Herman Race, I'm a licensed private investigator and I've been so since May of 1968. I specialize mostly in criminal matters. However, prior to my becoming an investigator, in 1968, I was a member of the New York City Police Department, since 1947. I served for a short time in the uniformed forces and then I became a member of the detective division. I was a member of the detective division for 18 years . . . 10 years as a detective and 8 years as supervisor of detectives. I reached first-grade detective, which today there are very few of them because it's sort of being eliminated from the department.

H: How did you get involved in the DeFeo Case?

R: Michael Brigante who is the father of the deceased, Louise DeFeo, personally asked me to conduct an investigation to determine what really took place on the night of the murders. Bill Weber went to the courts and got permission to retain me as an investigator because he was defending Ronnie DeFeo and he wanted to know what took place. So basically I was brought into the case from two different angles. My friendship of many years with Mike Brigante and of course, professionally, with Bill Weber.

H: Do you believe it's possible for one person to have committed the crime?

R: In my opinion, yes, it's possible. In this case I would say, not probable. It's my own honest opinion that Butch had an accomplice to commit this crime. It's my honest opinion that these murders were not committed by Butch, all by himself.

H: Why do you believe he had help?

R: I say it is almost inconceivable that the sound wouldn't wake somebody. However, if somebody was there to pacify the children, to say go back to sleep, it's only a dream, it's only a nightmare, or words to that effect, there's a strong possibility it happened that way.

H: Why do you think Ronnie killed?

R: He really and truly was under the belief that the family had formed a conspiracy and they were out to get him. That was his attitude, that in reality, to save his own life, it was necessary to take the lives of the family. And then he felt relieved.

H: You don't believe he was possessed or in demonology?

R: The only demons went through the house looking for money maybe, after the murders. I never saw anything to indicate this mystic phenomenon and all that nonsense. And I use that word nonsense 'cause that's exactly what it is, it's nonsense.

H: Why were the bodies all in the same position?

R: Well I've thought about that too, and as I say, it's very hard to explain. A very often asked question – was he able to commit these murders by himself. Well, there's a lot of pros and cons on that. This was nighttime. Six people were shot. How long it actually took . . . we're talking about a matter of minutes. And within those few minutes, as soon as the first shot went off, it's almost inconceivable that somebody wouldn't hear a sound.

* * *

William E. Weber is a powerful figure, quiet, soft-spoken, but very effective. I first met him in the winter of 1976 with Bernard Burton, his colleague, and was struck by his ability to ferret out some aspects of a testimony which might have escaped a less skillful interrogator.

H: Bill Weber, how did you get involved in the DeFeo case to begin with?

W: Well, I had been practicing criminal law for sometime in Suffolk County, and one of the judges who was then assigned to the case, Judge Signoreli, asked me to interview Ronnie with a view towards representing him. After interviewing him, Ronnie asked that I continue as his attorney.

H: When you first familiarized yourself with the case, did you think there was anything unusual about it, from your point of view?

W: Well, you're talking about the crime of the century as far as I'm concerned. Is it unusual for the eldest son of a middle class Italian family to wipe out his entire family, six members of the family? Of course it's unusual.

H: Why do you think he did it?

W: Why? That's a question I've asked all the experts, both during the trial and after the trial, and I haven't come up with the answer yet.

H: Did he do it?

W: Well, Ronnie said, to a certain extent, he participated in it.

H: Who else was in it, do you think?

A: We have no idea. Ronnie never explicitly said who was involved in it with him. But there are some theories on that.

H: Is there a possibility there might have been somebody else?

A: Yes.

H: Somebody Ronnie would have known?

A: Possibly.

H: Could it have been a member of the family?

A: Well, there has been one theory that one member of the family assisted him in some of the killings. I don't adhere to that theory.

H: Could Ronnie have done it alone?

W: I don't think it was possible that he did it alone.

H: Why?

W: You're talking about eight expertly placed bullets, by an individual who has been described by an optometrist as being almost legally blind; you're talking about an individual supposedly having executed this crime, this mass murder in the space of ten seconds, on two floors of a colonial home; and using a .35 Marlon rifle . . . I don't know if you're familiar with the percussion of a rifle like that, but I think everyone in Amityville should have heard these sounds of the bullets, but yet no one, not even the next door neighbor, John Nemeth, whose bedroom window was open and facing the DeFeo house, heard it. Taking all these factors together there's no way that I could imagine how one person could have committed the crime.

H: How do you explain the fact that no noise was heard?

W: I asked that question of every police expert that testified during the trial, particularly Sergeant Alfred Delapenna, who was the Suffolk County ballistics expert, a very learned gentleman, and he, together with all the other experts, *stated that they had no explanation.*

H: If there's no explanation in the ordinary way, there has to be an explanation in some other way. What about the possibility that the family might have been drugged?

W: No, there were autopsy reports and toxicology reports made on each of the victims. And in each case there was no evidence whatsoever of drugs or any other medication given to the victims.

H: Why do you think Ronnie would have killed his whole family?

W: I have no explanation of why Ronnie killed his whole family, if at all he did. There's been some definite evidence as to why he would want to kill his father, but how a boy who loved his mother, who adored and idolized his two younger brothers, could possibly do such a thing; to me, it was an act of insanity.

H: And if it weren't an act of insanity, we would have to look somewhere else for an explanation, since there is no logical explanation, wouldn't you think?

W: Well, I'm sure that some time in the future there's going to be a logical explanation. I don't want to adhere to any other unspoken explanation.

H: But you don't have an explanation as of now, do you?

W: No, I don't.

* * *

When I first read the long interrogatory between psychiatrist Dr Daniel Schwartz and the defendant, it was clear to me that Dr Schwartz matched Bill Weber in the width of his horizons – the very opposite of a pragmatic man like investigator Herman Race.

Having familiarized myself with the opinions put forth during the trial, I turned to Dr Schwartz with questions I thought might elicit some views of his concerning the marginal aspects of the case as seen from my point of view:

H: Dr Daniel Schwartz, you're a psychiatrist and you have been a specialist on criminal cases. What do you feel is the underlying cause that made DeFeo commit these crimes?

S: I don't know if I can give you an adequate, or even a complete picture. This was a young man who, from all we know, never really learned to control his emotions in a reasonable way. He grew up as a violent man, in a house of violence, and was filled with murderous thoughts and the paranoid idea that he was meant to be killed. And there came a time in his life when he felt that he had to kill others lest he be killed.

H: Do you feel he was not sane in the generally accepted sense at the time of the murders?

S: Yes, I believe that he was so psychotic at the time of the murders that he was not criminally responsible, that he was unable to understand the nature and quality of his acts and that they were wrong.

H: DeFeo claims that he wasn't at all murderous in his behavior prior to moving to the house at Ocean Avenue. Have you looked into that angle, as to his previous condition?

S: Yes, he had been violent before, as a youngster.

H: What about just before moving into the house, has he been violent at that time?

S: I can't give you exact dates at this moment, but I know all through his schooling, he was a difficult child. He had to be placed in one school after another, because he could not be managed in class.

H: Do you think that there is a possibility that some other underlying cause might have made him commit these crimes, other than what you have just suggested, that is to say, that he might be psychotic at the time of the murder. Do you think he might be the recipient of some extraordinary influences in the house?

S: I don't know. *I have an open mind about things like this*. I just don't know. There are aspects of the case that cannot be explained from a psychiatric point of view, as far as we know, and there are many aspects that I think can be.

H: Have you seen him since he has been committed to Dannemora?

S: No.

H: Have you had any reports concerning his current condition?

S: No.

H: Do you feel that he might change again, being now isolated from the house of crime?

S: He might change, I don't know if it's the result of isolation from the house of crime or if it's a result of separation from his family. I don't mean it facetiously, the family is dead. He spoke about other people being on his list, people that he had to kill, people who represented a danger to him. But I think it's significant that the only people he did kill, as far as we know, were his immediate family. The interesting thing is that this boy who was at times quite violent, apparently at the time of this crime, acted in a very calm way, and there are parts of it that he has no knowledge about, no real awareness of himself moving about or getting from one place to another, suggesting that there was a strong degree of *dissociation* during the crime.

* * *

Naturally, by now the house of horrors was much more in the public eye than the poor fellow serving life in Dannemora. When I use these terms I am not for a minute trying to whitewash him of his crime, but to have compassion even for a man in prison is, I feel, humane and proper. Nobody ever leaves prisons like Dannemora a better man. If anything, he harbors more hatred that what he might have had when he went inside.

But as the house had become the center of people's interest, I went to see the curator of the Amityville museum run by the local historical Society, which I thought would be a repository of useful – and accurate – information regarding the house, the area and land, and anything pertaining to the rapidly expanding legend of the *Amityville Horror* novel.

I already knew that the townspeople were anything but overjoyed with the whole subject, but I hoped I might be able to elicit some additional facts from the curator. Here is the record of our meeting, exactly as it occurred in July of 1979:

H: Mr Seth Purdy, you are the curator of the Amityville Historical Society?

P: That's right.

H: How many years have you been in this position?

P: About four.

H: You are familiar, of course, with the house on Ocean Avenue, which has been the center of some pretty dramatic fiction over the last year or so. I believe there was another house that once stood on that spot. Can you tell me about that?

P: I, myself am not aware of that other house. I only know about the house that's presently there.

H: Well, the house that's presently there was there only for 108 years. Prior to that there was another house, which is now at the corner of Carmen St and South Island Place in this town. Since you've been curator here, have you had any occasion to research the house in any way.

P: No, I have not researched the house.

H: With all the excitement of motion pictures and books, have you looked into the background on the house, to the best of your knowledge, is there anything historically interesting connected with that house.

P: No, I have not looked into the background of the house.

H: How do you feel about some of the, shall we say, unusual happenings being reported from there?

P: Well, I simply do not believe them.

H: Well, have you had any personal experiences at the house, have you been to that house at any time?

P: No, I have not.

H: Do you know of anybody who might have worked with you or might have confided in you, who had been, in fact, to the house?

P: No, I do not.

H: How do you view all this excitement in terms of, shall we say, tourist traffic and general attention to the town?

P: I think it's interesting and this places the community on the map, but I don't know whether it's of value or not.

H: How do you feel in general about such matters, shall we say, psychic research, parapsychology and the investigation of unusual human phenomena?

P: I have no belief or faith in that at all.

H: Do you think it's a matter of belief or faith?

P: I would feel so.

H: You don't think it's a matter of collecting evidence then?

P: No.

H: What about this old house that is now at a corner several blocks away from the present location, at Carmen and South Island Place, are you aware of such a house?

P: No I am not.

H: It seems interesting that a 200-year-old house shouldn't come to the attention of the Historical Society.

P: Well, only if we were researching the houses at the present time, but we're not.

H: Are there a lot of 200-year-old houses in this community?

P: There are probably several of them.

H: And they're of no great interest to you?

P: Yes, they are of interest. But it's a project and

financial matter to research, and therefore we have not done it.

H: Have you any knowledge of the area in which the house at 112 Ocean Avenue is currently standing?

P: I know where the area is, of course I've been there.

H: Mr Purdy, what sort of Indians used to live around here?

P: In the area where Amityville is presently located, it was part of the holdings of the Massapequa Indian tribe, which was one of the 13 original tribes of Long Island.

H: Were they a very large nation?

P: No, very small. I don't even know if a hundred.

H: Are there any Indians in the area still?

P: Not to my knowledge, no.

H: Where would these Indians have lived in this particular area?

P: The Massapequa Indians lived in the community that today is called Massapequa, on the shores of the Great South Bay, in an area now known as Harbor Green.

H: What about Amityville township, in town where were the houses now are?

P: No Indians were at any time living in this area.

H: Three hundred years ago, no Indians?

P: No, not to my knowledge.

H: Not to your knowledge. What about Shawnees, were there any in this area?

P: No. I believe these Indians were members of the Algonquin tribe.

H: Well, there seem to be some indication that there were Shawnee Indians which, as you probably know, went all the way down to Brooklyn, New York at one point, also lived in this area, in a minority position. Is any of this known to you?

P: Not to my knowledge, no.

H: Mr Purdy, are there any other Indians connected with this area apart from the Massapequa Indians?

P: In the Amityville area?

H: General area, yes.

P: Not to my knowledge.

H: What about the Shinnegcocks?

P: The Shinnegcocks are on the Eastern end of Long Island, and as far as I know they may be descendants of the original Long Island Indians, but a recent name . . . by recent, maybe a hundred years.

H: In this area or north of here or where?

P: East of this area, about 90 miles to the east.

H: Was there ever any Indian burial ground discovered in this general area?

P: Not to my knowledge. The only story I've ever heard of any Indian being buried in that area, was south of the house that you're discussing, and it was reported that they had discovered the skeleton of an Indian chief. Indicated that was a chief because he was in a standing position.

H: Whereabout did that happen?

P: On Ocean Avenue, *about quarter of a mile south of the house that you've talked about.*

H: And what happened to the skeleton?

P: I don't know.

H: But there is in fact a skeleton? There was in fact a skeleton at one time?

P: Was, yes.

6

A Visit With Ronald DeFeo, Jr At Dannemora

For a while, the fruit of my investigation lay dormant on the shelf, partly because we did not go any further with any publications of the amazing things I had discovered, and partly because of a sensational new book written by a gentleman until then known primarily for documentaries who had never written a book before. By chance or through the cleverness of its editor, the book became a best seller, and while this pleased those who were responsible for it, it did not please the George Lutz family very much. At this writing, there are several law suits going on between them and their former attorneys, between them and the newspaper which first published the account of their trials and tribulations, and lastly but not least, between the current owners of the house and the Lutz's, the publishers of the book dealing with their account, and American International Pictures, for making a motion picture based upon the book. If it all sounds like a three-ring circus or a French farce, it is, because none of these law suits are likely to end up with any substance. But it does illustrate the high tide of emotions which the case has engendered in people, and the state of affairs in the little town of Amityville, where such matters have never happened before. The house was eventually sold to a couple named Cromarty, who went to great lengths to discount the entire story of the whole thing, and announced through the press that their house was beautiful and not haunted. What it was haunted by, it soon developed, was a hoard of unwelcome tourists from all over, who came to look at the house, but frequently rang the Cromarty's door bell, or made other attempts to invade the privacy. One cannot truly blame either the new owners of the house or the people of Amityville for being annoyed by the whole thing, for the curiosity of tourists can be a very upsetting thing. On the other hand, it happened and hostility toward basically naive and innocent strangers isn't going to enhance the image of Amityville to the world. Recently the house was finally sold to an enterprising gentleman from the Deep South, for the original price of $80,000, and this seems like a logical conclusion of what the entire case turned into. As I understand it the gentleman will turn the house into a tourist attraction, although he may have to do this somewhere else than in Amityville. It seems pretty likely that the Amityville authorities are not about to permit such a venture but then again, if London Bridge can prosper in the Arizona desert, so can the Amityville House somewhere else. It will be completely free from evil influences, if it is moved somewhere else, whereas the spot where it presently stands will not be. However, that is another story.

In the spring of 1979, I was approached by an Allentown, Pennsylvania television production company, Armstrong Productions, with the thought of doing a documentary on the real story of Amityville. The idea appealed to me, especially as so much of the false story had already been published. What the company, headed by Warren Armstrong, had in mind was for their producer, John Nicick and their director Andrew Wiesner, to help me put together a half-hour program for television entitled 'Murder in Amityville' in which the entire evidence would be looked at afresh, but without prejudice and including the point of view of a parapsychologist such as I. This seemed to me the only way to bring some sort of reasonable balance into what had become a largely distorted picture of the events. To begin with, I knew already that the house was heavily haunted in the classical sense of the term. But there were other such houses all over the world, no better or worse. The DeFeo murder tragedy was unusual in that six people died simultaneously, and that a member of their own family was accused of doing it. But again, horrid crimes do occur from time to time in various places and are not necessarily unique. What made this case outstanding, however, was the possibility of possession by alien, external entities that were causing the young murderer to act as he did. With this possibility in mind, I then proceeded to put together the story of the television program, and together we pursued it to the best of our ability. In three hectic days of filming, we managed to interview some of the most important people involved, and on June 27, 1979, I personally interviewed the most important person of all, Ronald DeFeo, Jr himself. To do so, it took a great deal of string pulling on the part of attorney William Weber, but eventually we were allowed the visit. Our crew, however, was denied access to the penitentiary at Dannemora, New York, and only Mr Weber and I, the sole survivors of this large enterprise, were finally permitted inside the stern gates of this maximum security prison. Before we were allowed to enter the inner precincts themselves, we went through a thorough search of our persons, had to leave metallic objects behind, and even my nose drops were heavily scrutinized and finally held back by the guard who suspected that it might in some way be useful to the inmates.

After some more waiting, Bill Weber and I met with Ronald DeFeo in a small room inside the prison complex; two guards remained outside, looking at us all the time through a small window. In a sense I did not resent this, since I felt they were looking out for our safety as well. What follows is the verbatim interview I conducted with Ronald DeFeo in person, and it is very revealing, particularly toward the end when I attempted to put him under hypnosis and failed, due to what Ronnie called 'them' not wanting me to do so.

June 27, 1979.

Q: When you go back into your childhood, did you have at any time any kind of psychic experiences or ESP experiences or feelings of a paranormal nature?

A: No, not that I recall.

Q: Did you ever have dreams about things that later became reality?

A: Not really, no. That became reality, no.

Q: Were you ever interested in things like psychic phenomena, or ghosts, ESP and that sort of thing?

A: I hinted around—

Q: Did you ever read anything about it?

A: Yes, plenty.

Q: What sort of books have you read?

A: I don't remember the names; it was a long time ago, when I was in high school.

Q: Before you lived in the house at 112 Ocean Avenue. Where did you live before that?

A: Foster Avenue, in Brooklyn.

Q: Did anything unusual happen to you there, like having foreknowledge, or a feeling that something might happen?

A: Not really, no.

Q: Did you ever have a feeling when you met somebody that you've met them before? When, in fact, you didn't?

A: That has happened quite a number of times.

Q: Will you give me an example?

A: Well, I met somebody in Brooklyn, when I moved to Foster Avenue, that I thought lived in the other neighborhood; it looked alike, but it wasn't the same person.

Q: When you first moved into 112 Ocean Avenue in Amityville, what was your impression of the house? The first time you set foot in it?

A: It was a big thing coming out of an apartment; a new experience, you know. It was like day and night.

Q: Did you get any feeling, any uncanny feeling? Any feeling of doom, or anything unpleasant, or any feeling of fear in the house? Did you feel anything at all about the atmosphere of the house?

A: Well, when I first moved in, you know, you start hearing noises and different things at night.

Q: How long after you moved in?

A: As soon as I moved in.

Q: First day?

A: Yes.

Q: First night?

A: Yes.

Q: What exactly did you hear the first night?

A: You know – the floors, noise – you felt as though somebody might have been walking around, pipes banging, all these strange noises. In fact, everybody thought there was somebody in there a week after we moved in.

Q: Did you check whether there were any burglars?

A: Yeah, they checked that; they checked everything all out. Closets, everything.

Q: Now, when you first set foot in the house, the first day, did you have any feelings about the house?

A: I thought it was a nice house; I thought things were going to work out right.

Q: You didn't have any unusual premonitions or feelings of any kind? How about at night; the first night you slept in the house?

A: It was a little weird getting adjusted to it.

Q: Did you hear anything the first night?

A: I heard a lot of things the first night.

Q: What did you hear?

A: You know, like noise in the middle of the night; sort of banging.

Q: How did you respond to it?

A: I got up. I wanted to know what it was.

Q: What did you find? Did you find anything?

A: I didn't find anything.

Q: Did you tell anyone about it?

A: Yes, they were up walking around, too; the members of my family.

Q: They didn't see anything, either?

A: No.

Q: Now did you ever, during the time you lived in the house, see anything that was unusual?

A: Well, I never *saw* anything that was unusual.

Q: Did you ever hear anything?

A: Yeah, I heard a lot of things.

Q: Can you tell me what you heard?

A: Once in awhile, you'd hear screaming, but there wasn't nobody screaming.

Q: Male or female?

A: Both.

Q: Did you ever have a strange dream in the house?

A: Not really.

Q: Did you ever see any objects move by themselves? Or things disappear and reappear?

A: I never saw anything disappear and reappear. I never saw anything move, but there was things moved. Who moved them, to this day, I don't know.

Q: Could you describe it?

A: Well, somebody moved a painting from the first floor to the second floor in the middle of the night.

Q: How long after you moved in?

A: Maybe in '70 or '71.

Q: What was the painting of?

A: It was my grandfather's painting, come to think of it.

Q: It was moved?

A: It was moved from the second floor to the third floor.

Q: By nobody in the family?

A: No, everybody asked each other, if anybody had moved it. I didn't move it; everybody else said they didn't. I thought it was somebody just playing games.

Q: Did you get any feelings about all these things when they kept happening? What did you think of it?

A: What did I think of it? I thought somebody was honestly playing games.

Q: Who did you think was playing games?

A: Well, I'll be honest with you. My mother and father both played a lot of games.

Q: Did they, in fact, do this?

A: I don't know. I really don't know, because when I started getting over that age, later on, I just didn't come home a lot of times. Most of the time, I didn't even live in the house, to be honest with you.

Q: Did your family members report anything unusual to you in that way?

A: They were always saying somebody is in the house; ghosts, all that.

Q: Did any of them ever see any?

A: I recall my mother or somebody at one time said they saw something. But what it was, I never got into with them.

Q: She said she saw a ghost?

A: Not a ghost.

Q: An apparition?

A: They felt the devil was in the house, to be honest

with you. That's what brought all the religion into the house.

Q: During the time you lived there, they brought a priest into the house, I believe?

A: He slept there.

Q: Did it do any good?

A: I don't know because, to be honest with you, when he came, I left.

Q: You didn't think he could do any good?

A: No. Me and him were sleeping on the same floor; it was the extra room up there, and I just left.

Q: Now, tell me this. When did you hear what you call voices talking to you, for the first time?

A: Did I hear voices?

Q: Yes.

A: I'll be honest with you. I never heard any voices. The voices I heard and told you about in the house – the screaming and stuff.

Q: Did you ever hear a voice telling you to do certain things?

A: Me? No.

Q: Nobody told you to kill. No one ever told you anything like that. Because that is in the—

A: I know, it's in the testimony.

Q: Why is it in the testimony?

A: Because I tried to convince the psychiatrist that I was insane.

Q: You're not insane?

A: I don't feel I am.

Q: Why did you feel that talking about a voice . . .

A: I had to convince the psychiatrist I was crazy before I could go before the court and convince a jury.

Q: But saying that you heard voices doesn't prove insanity.

A: No, it isn't, but I felt it was.

Q: That night, when you came home, and the murder took place, did you feel that you were acting under duress? Did you feel that you were being influenced by anyone? An unseen force?

A: Well, I'll be honest with you, when I shot my mother – no, I shot my father first, then I crossed over and went to my mothe 's bed and shot her. After that, I'll tell you honestly, I couldn't stop if I wanted to. There was no way I could stop. I couldn't put the gun down.

Q: Did you feel that somebody else was moving your hands in any way?

A: *I felt somebody was inside moving me.*

Q: Was that the first time that ever happened?

A: The first that had ever happened?

Q: When you felt anybody inside you?

A: No, no, no. I've felt like *I was somebody else sometimes*, you know.

Q: Let's talk about that. When did that first happen? How far back?

A: I think it was in '70 or '71.

Q: In the house?

A: Yeah, in the house.

Q: How did you notice the difference between this other personality and yourself?

A: Well, I always had respect towards my father; he was violent, had a bad temper. I've always had to respect him. I know that I could beat him, but not with my hands, but there was other ways to beat him. I'd thought about it, but I'd never taken my thought and went ahead with it, and one day I picked up the shotgun, I knew the gun was loaded and I said 'the hell with it.' I just cocked it and went to kill him, but the gun didn't go off.

Q: What made you do it? Did you feel it was another person inside you?

A: It's very possible.

Q: Did you ever feel an alien personality inside you? Like somebody who wasn't really you, in other words, doing something you didn't want to do? The conflict between you and that other person?

A: Oh, I've felt that way. Yes and no.

Q: But did you ever hear this person talk to you or give you thoughts?

A: I can't say he talked to me, like me sitting here now, talking to you.

Q: No, not that way; in your mind!

A: In my mind, yes.

Q: Did you ever hear that?

A: Yeah, plenty of times.

Q: What did this other thing – what were the thoughts that this person conveyed to you?

A: Like, before I killed my family, maybe you shouldn't do it, you know? It tried to talk me out of it and then somethin' tried to talk me into it, back and forth the ball went.

Q: Now, the thing that talked you into it, what did it sound like?

A: That's hard to explain. It seems to be my own voice talking to me, but it's not talking.

Q: Is it left side or right side?

A: I'd say right in the middle; they're all over, you know?

Q: Did this other personality give you new ideas; what you should or shouldn't do?

A: I did have the idea of killing – not only my own family, the Brigante family and DeFeo family, that same night. What made me stop, I could not tell you, because to this day I feel I should have killed them all.

Q: Why do you feel you should have done that? Does this voice tell you that? This inside person.

A: Well, I will say this. Inside, I feel you should never start something you can't finish. When I sit down to think about it—

Q: Did you ever have these feelings in any other house? Apart from 112 Ocean Avenue?

A: No.

Q: Always in that one house? In other words, you might meet members of the family outside and not have those feelings.

A: *No, it seemed to be the whole problem originated and ended in that house.*

Q: You never heard this person say something to you like do this or do that, nudging you like it came from you and yet not from you? Do you understand? What other ideas did this entity give you? Did you ever have the feeling that somebody was trying to tell you that something was wrong with the house or something happened on that spot, or anything like that? Have you ever had any thoughts about that coming to you out of nowhere?

A: You mean, like something you would say and I'd already know you were going to come out with?

Q: Yes.

A: Plenty of times.

Q: About the house, for instance.

A: Well, somebody – one of my friends – I don't know if he was joking or what, but I knew he was going to come with something off the wall about something that did happen in the house, and sure enough, he told my mother that somebody was just murdered in the house – somebody was murdered or killed in the house, something like that.

Q: He said that?

A: Yes.

Q: Is this before all these things took place?

A: Yes. His name is Barry Springer. He's still alive. We were just talking about it the other day with me – very recently – last year.

Q: He came to the house and he said to your mother, 'Somebody was murdered in this house'?

A: Yeah, that's what he told my mother, because we were making a joke out of it out here around home.

Q: When you were actually doing the shooting, did you have a feeling like you were a zombie? Like a machine? As if you were not in control of yourself?

A: Oh, there's no doubt about it; I was out of control after the first two killings.

Q: When did it end?

A: Oh, it ended quick. As far as I remember, I was just standing there with the rifle, and I said, 'Oh,' and it was over with.

Q: How about your sister? Did she do any of the killing with you?

A: No, I did it all.

Q: You had a very close, telepathic relationship with your sister. Did you think she read your thoughts at any time, and vice versa?

A: She knew a lot of times what I was capable of doing. She knew that I had certain things on my mind and probably did them; she couldn't prove it, but she—

Q: Did she ever tell you about it?

A: She told me about it a number of times.

Q: Now, some of these things that happened, either here or before you came here, even in dreams or what seems to be dreams, have you ever seen or heard your dead family members?

A: No. Since this happened? No.

Q: Have you heard that inner voice that you heard before, that inner prompting, has that been with you since that time?

A: It still comes back now and then.

Q: What does it tell you?

A: What does it tell me? Like this meeting here – I knew this was going to take place. It was just a matter of time; I couldn't pinpoint that.

Q: That I would come to you?

A: Either you or somebody else. Not you, in general, but somebody else.

Q: How did you know that?

A: Because in my own mind, you know, I would be sitting down, thinking, and a voice would – not a voice – you know, myself – I feel that something is going to break; it's just a matter of time, now, it's coming. The last time I got this feeling, I got a letter in the mail from Gloria Springer. She came up here, too. Somebody I didn't even know, wanted to write a book.

Q: Did you ever know things before they happen? Would you say that you have a degree of clairvoyance about things before they happen?

A: Well, like this letter. I'll say, 'I'm not going to get a letter today, but I'm gonna get one tomorrow' and sure enough, I got it tomorrow. Things like that, yeah.

Q: What is your attitude toward parapsychology, let us say psychic phenomena, survival of human personality beyond death? What is your attitude toward these things? What do you believe?

A: Well, I've never really been into it. I believe that it's all very possible. I don't believe that it's all just a bunch of lies.

Q: What do you feel about, let us say, when you pass on to the next stage of existence; how do you feel you will be received over there when you meet your dead relatives?

A: Honestly, I believe when you're dead, you're dead and that's it. They put you into the ground or they cremate you or whatever they want to do, and that's it.

Q: You don't think there will be a survival beyond that?

A: I honestly don't think so.

Q: Did your father believe it?

A: Oh, sure. He believed in Heaven and Hell, the Devil, God and all that.

Q: So you have no fears?

A: Towards things like that, no.

Q: Did you hear any shots at the time you were doing the actual shooting yourself?

A: I'll be honest with you; the noise was so tremendous my ears were ringing. But there's one thing I did hear – I heard a dog barking. I heard a dog screaming, in fact, but it wasn't my dog. It apparently was a dog outside, and the gunshots must have been so sensitive that it affected that dog and that dog is part of what covered up the shots that I was putting off. I never realized this at the time, but today, later on, I realize it.

Q: When you were doing the shooting, did any of them know they were being shot?

A: No. It happened so quick. I mean, it was boom, boom, boom. From the first killing to the last, it never took any longer than seven seconds, it would be a lot, that would have been a lot. Seven seconds.

Q: Purely logically speaking, was there any reason you should have killed them?

A: No.

Q: So, since you had no reason, do you think something got into you to make you do it?

A: For what I did here, yes. Definitely. Something; there is no doubt about it in my mind.

Q: What do you think did it?

A: To tell you the truth, I don't know, because I loved my family. I tell you, to this day, I did not hate any of them. None of them. Especially them kids. I shot my brother. There was no call for that, and there is no doubt in my mind – I could see my temper going if I had been high on drugs or drunk, killing my mother – I mean killing my father – never going for my mother, but I did. That I can live with, *but it is still hard for me to wonder why I killed them.*

Q: You were not on drugs at the time?

A: During them killings, no. I had a little whiskey in me, but—

Q: You did say to your father at one time, when you ran away and you were brought back, that he should let you go; otherwise, you'd kill him.

A: I told him that a long time ago.

Q: What made you say that?

A: To tell you the truth, I don't know. Sometimes words just come out and I don't mean for them to come out. It's not even in my chain of thought, but they just come out. Boom, you know strange things, you know – I think about those things.

Q: You know how to define possession. Now, even though you have no belief in the survival of human personality as you have said, do you feel, from what you know, and what I've said, that there may have been some sort of possession by an entity other than yourself within you?

A: *Within me, yeah.* I would go with that 100%. Apparently, there is.

Q: Well, who do you think was this thing within you?

A: I really don't believe in God and I don't believe in the Devil, but if such exists, and my father had all that God in the house, it's very possible it could have been the Devil. If they all, like I say, really does exist.

Q: Were you ever interested in American Indians?

A: No, not really.

Q: Did you know that the house was built on an Indian burial ground?

A: No, I did not know that.

Q: When you moved into the house, did you have any knowledge of anyone having had trouble in this spot before? There were some strange stories about the land, weren't there?

A: I don't know. I never paid much attention. I know there were a lot of stories.

Q: A recurrent dream is when you have the same dream more than once or twice, and it comes back. Did you ever have any recurrent dreams?

A: No, I'll be honest with you, I don't dream too much. No. I've woken up out of a dead sleep and felt something was going to happen, and it happened.

Q: What, for instance?

A: I was with some young lady, in her apartment, you know, and I had a dream that somebody was going to come and try to do something to me; that's what I felt, anyway. When I did get up, the door was open, and the guy was coming in. I stopped him. Whether or not he was going to do anything – I never let it get that far to find out. I just put a stop to it quick.

Q: How?

A: Well, I'll be honest with you, I can't say how, but he'll never hurt anybody again.

Q: Did you ever have a dream in which you thought you had another family or that you had a secret wife and children?

A: I've dreamed that my mother and father weren't my mother and father – I don't know about the other family. I couldn't belong to another family.

Q: How old were you at that time?

A: That still happens to this day. It's nothing new.

Q: This happened before the murder?

A: Oh, yeah, I just feel – I know what I am, and I'm different from anybody in this family that's still alive.

Q: How different?

A: You know, entirely different, because they feel that you should go out in the street, you should get a job, you should go to college, or take something you like, fine and dandy. That's for them, but that's not for me, you know? The way they live, and what they want to do and how they want to eat – it's like a pair of shoes, either they fit or they don't fit.

Q: You mean you felt a stranger in your own family?

A: Yeah, I felt like I was a stranger in my own family, yes.

Q: Do you know anything about that other secret family; what they were like and what you were like? Did you ever see yourself?

A: No, I never saw myself. I just felt that I was out of place. Just felt I didn't belong there.

Q: Did you on occasion say that you had a wife and children?

A: Maybe I did. I don't recall.

Q: Now, since this all happened, do you feel regret, or what do you feel about your position? Do you feel that you did it consciously, do you feel that it just happened? What is your own attitude toward this?

A: Before, killings, spot killings bother me to this day. What I mean they bother me, I don't understand myself, what got into me. This I cannot understand; the one, my father, I can understand.

Q: You didn't get on with your father?

A: I knew some day it was going to come to a head; either he was going to kill me or I was going to kill him. I knew this was coming, and he knew it was coming, and it was no secret from anybody.

Q: Did you have that feeling before you moved into this house or after, about your father?

A: No, after. After. Not right away, but afterwards. It was not a day or a week; I'd say – I couldn't even quote the time – it could be a year or two years.

Q: Do you think you had a personality change after you moved to 112 Ocean Avenue?

A: *There's no doubt about it.*

Q: Describe the difference between the pre-112 and after you moved in. How was your personality different?

A: Well, *when I moved there, I started getting cold and vicious inside*, but I would not bring it out and let people see it; I would let the people see the opposite, a coward, you know. I would not let the people know that inside I was vicious and capable of killing; I would not let them know that. I wanted them to think the complete opposite which I did make them think.

Q: Did this happen after you moved into the house?

A: Yeah.

Q: Did it ever occur to you to wonder why the change in your personality took place when you moved to 112?

A: I've thought about it, but never came up with an answer.

Q: Your father had said 'I have a devil on my back.' What do you think he meant by that?

A: Me.

Q: You were the devil?

A: Yeah. That's what he said.

Q: You don't believe in the devil?

A: I tell you the truth, today, I don't know what to believe in, anymore.

Q: What about that little red room downstairs?

A: All that was; I'm going to be honest with you, was a storage closet.

Q: I believe you. I want you to relax completely. Close your eyes. Listen to my voice coming to you from a distance. I want you to make your mind a blank as I speak to you. Tune in on me. Tune into my voice and nothing else. You're to relax for the next few minutes, to let go completely. Unclasp your hands, please, relax your body. Listen to my voice coming to you, as I count to ten. One, two, three, four, five, six, seven, eight, nine, ten. You're going to let go more and more; your body feels very relaxed. Your body feels very light and now you become more and more relaxed. You will not awaken until I waken you by calling your name and you will hear every word I speak. As you take a short rest, you're taking ten more steps down – one, two, three, four, five, six, seven, eight, nine, ten – let go completely. You're floating, floating, your body feels lighter and lighter, as you go down ten more steps. One, two, three, four, five, six, seven, eight, nine, ten. You will not awaken until I waken you. You will hear every word I speak, you will keep your eyes closed until I awaken you. I will ask you some questions which you must answer truthfully, even though asleep, but you will stay asleep until I waken you. Sleep now. Rest completely. Quietly, peacefully. I want you to go back in time now. You are just 20 years old. Just go back in time.

A: Something inside of me won't let you hypnotize me.

Q: What is the something inside you?

A: I don't know. Something inside just saying, 'It won't work; go on, it won't work.'

Q: What happened when I started counting?

A: I was relaxed; I was almost asleep.

Q: All right. Let me try it again. Only this time we'll talk to the something inside you and it will work.

A: I don't know.

Q: Try again, please. Go down again. One, two, three, four, five, six, seven, eight, nine, ten. Go down deeper. Go down again, as you had before. One, two, three, four, five, six, seven, eight, nine, ten. I am appealing to the entity within you, and appealing to the Chief of the Indians who has control of you. Please, please, let go of this man now. Please, we honor you, please, let him speak to us, and let him tell us the truth. When I awaken him, I want him to tell us the truth about you, please. Please identify yourself; tell us who you are. We respect and honor you; we come as your friends. One, two, three, four, five, six, seven, eight, nine, ten. At the count of ten, I will awaken you. One, two, three, four, five, six, seven, eight, nine, ten. Ronnie, awaken.

A: I wakened myself, don't worry.

Q: What did you feel when I spoke?

A: A voice. It's not a voice – it's not a feeling. *It's just a feeling inside saying no way will we let you hypnotize us.*

Q: Who do you think they were? You say 'we' will let you hypnotize us.

A: I don't know. It's a feeling I get a lot.

Q: You don't know who they are that speak that way?

A: No. Sometimes I get like that. My mind gets made up for me inside, and I just got to go with it and live with it, *and whatever it says, I have to do.*

Q: Is there more than one person that controls you? You say 'we'.

A: No. I feel it's my inner self. Just like a lot of times I want to do something to someone because I'm mad, and I shouldn't do it because normally I wouldn't; something inside me says don't do it, and I know I could do it; I keep working at it and I could take somebody in my hands and take their life.

Q: Do you mean to say that Ronald DeFeo is not always in charge of Ronald DeFeo?

A: No. I'm not always in charge of myself, no. I'm not using that as an excuse to try to get out of what I done, *but I'm not in charge of myself all the time.*

Q: That isn't the reason I asked it. I asked point blank: Is there something within you that comes, from time to time, to control you? An entity within yourself?

A: I would say so; something inside me.

Q: As different from your usual self?

A: Yeah. Quite. It's different. I want to do something and I won't do it. The more and more I think about it, the madder I get and want to do it, but can't. It's like somebody holding me back.

Q: On the other hand, does something make you do something you don't want to do? The ordinary you doesn't want to do?

A: Yeah. Definitely.

Q: You mean there is something within you at times that makes you do something against your will?

A: Yes. It definitely makes me do something against my will. I want to do something and the thing stops me from doing it.

Q: But what about making you do something that you would ordinarily not do? The other way around, in other words?

A: That happens, too. I wouldn't ordinarily just kill my brothers and sisters or any children, in fact, to be honest with you, but I did.

Q: Did you feel that this strange power within you has made you do it?

A: I would think so. I would say yes.

* * *

Almost two years after my visit to the house at 112 Ocean Ave., Amityville, with medium Ethel Johnson Meyers I returned to the town, again in her company, and that of my associates who were working with me on a documentary for television.

We were unable to enter the house itself; the current owners (or rather the people who just sold the house again) named Cromarty, who had stated to the press again and again that the house was nice and beautiful and free of anything supernatural, were in evidence in the garden, and it was clear we were not welcome.

When our television crew tried to film the house from across the street, they were actively interfered with by a young man from a house standing in back of the street corner.

Naturally, we did not get into an argument even though we had a perfect right to film on public property (the street) and had previously cleared our visit with local police and the Mayor. We just came back the next day and did what we came for when there was no one around to bother us.

But as the original seance had been held in the house itself, I was doubtful that a trance session elsewhere would have much value. On the other hand, it might be interesting to see whether the victims were now free spirits, in which case they could be contacted anywhere, not just in the house. We decided to make an attempt to do just that in the offices of attorney William Weber. Here is the record of what was obtained at that time in July, 1979:

H: Ethel Meyers, you and I have worked together many

times, you as a medium, I as an investigator. It is now midnight, you're in Long Island, I would like you to try to go into a trance, and see if anyone will come through to speak to us about this case which we have been investigating since 1975. Would you please close your eyes and relax completely and put yourself in whatever state you feel is most conducive to have any external entities speak through your vocal chords in trance. Let them come, whoever they might be.
(silence)

You can speak. Whoever you are, please speak.

E: Yes, Albert!

H: Good evening, Albert. I welcome you in these rather unusual circumstances. We would like your cooperation in exploring some of the unusual aspects of this case. What happened to the boy?

E: One night the pony, in jumping a fence, stumbled and fell and the boy was killed under the pony.

H: How is he connected with the house that was later moved or stood on this spot?

E: The Indian who was the great chieftain has an attendant who worshipped him, and anybody that would disturb even the bones of the great Indian chief was marked for death.

H: Now when the DeFeo family moved into this house which stood on the same spot, what exactly happened to young DeFeo to make him do what he did?

E: Under the control of this fierce young Indian, he was able to go forth with his gun and without sound kill each member.

H: Then do I understand correctly that because of the ancient wrong of having misused a skull, the Indian, angry at what has been done to him, decided to hurt those who live in the house after that?

E: That is part of it. He wanted this boy, right now, to again suffer the tortures that were coming to him because of his disrespect for the great chieftain.

H: What about after the killing? What happened to the spirits of those who had so suddenly been dispatched from one dimension into another. Do you feel them still in the house?

E: No.

H: Where are they now?

E: On the side of what you call heaven.

H: Can you see them?

E: I have seen them. They are learning and are not taking this in any way to hold them back.

H: Would you please explain from your side of the fence, what exactly happened and why it happened.

E: I have to go back to the turn of the century, into 1800, and at this time this young man was about 12 years of age. His father owned the property and he was about to dig a well to get water for his cattle in a more convenient place. The young man watching the proceedings suddenly sees bones turning up, and then a standing figure, and he removed the skull.

H: Now, the boy found a skull is that it?

E: Yes, on the standing skeleton.

H: And what did he do with it?

E: He took it home and scrubbed it up, made it clean, and then he put a candle in the skull and he went forth on his little pony, with a lighted candle in this skull, in the middle of the night to frighten everybody he knew in the township.

H: Now, if these people are free spirits on the other side, is there anything left in the house now that might conveniently or possibly be felt, seen or in other ways, be observed by those who are now in the house?

E: No, they have not returned, they have not disturbed anybody.

H: Then the house is clear?

E: The house is completely clear.

H: And what about young DeFeo, is he free from the influences of these evil spirits?

E: He is positively under their influence, particularly of the Indian.

H: Even now?

E: Even now, he is under his control and he is not his normal self.

* * *

With so much talk of the devil, demons and other unmentionable evil in that house (stuff of which great box office figures are made), and the fictionalizing of the account of George and Kathy Lutz in the bestselling book about it, I placed a call to George Lutz in San Diego. I had spoken with him on several occasions and always found him a pleasant, relaxed and polite man.

I came quickly to the point: what did he personally

believe was behind the troubles in his former home? I knew he had been critical of the book before, so wondered if he still felt that way. But George Lutz now seemed to be satisfied for some reason, he thought that the book and the film presented an 'accurate picture' of the events. Of course, I realized that he was about to embark on a tour helping to promote the film, a perfectly reasonable thing to do for anyone who has a piece of the action.

Did he believe there was some agency other than a spirit, even if evil, causing the phenomena? George was quite firm on that point. His religion, he explained to me – he had by now converted to Roman Catholicism, his wife's death – assured him that the Devil was real, that demons existed, and while he himself did not think they were real figures, he did feel that evil personified – an evil force of some kind, lurked in the house – not just a former human being with evil intents or acting in anger beyond the grave. I thought it therefore of some pertinence to speak with an authority on religion, especially of the Roman Catholic faith, and invited an eminent professor of theology at St Joseph's University, in Philadelphia, Dr Thomas McFadden, to discuss the matter with me.

Here is what transpired between Dr McFadden and myself on the subject of the devil and his minions:

Q: How would you define what is the devil, and what are demons? From your point of view?

A: From my point of view I think demons and devils are simply the personifications of evil forces that people have come to experience. I can't absolutely deny the existence of the devil but I certainly personally don't believe in a fallen angel who's become a devil. Nor do I believe in demon possession. Although that's been a classical doctrine of the church and theology over the centuries.

Q: How do you feel about possession when the possessed clearly has a totally new personality and especially when the personality is that of a deceased person, not otherwise known to the possessee.

A: I can't really explain it. I would have to leave that to the psychiatrist to explain. If the psychiatrist says that there is, or someone says that one possible explanation for this is possession by an evil spirit, I wouldn't be able to exclude that. I see certain dangers, and the danger I see is that it would preclude adequate medical treatment, that he would attribute it to an outside, supernatural force. The other danger would be that you might forget that the source of evil that human beings encounter is really deep, deep within them and it's easy to get human beings off the hook by simply attributing it to an outside force. What do you think?

Q: In the traditional view a distinction is made between the devil, Satan, whatever his names, and demons. Now, you and I know that the word demon really means 'spirit' in Greek. But, why do you suppose that the distinction has always been made between the devil as an individual, the anti-Christ, and demons? Why is there need for those two classes?

A: In traditional church teaching the distinction has been made between the devil, who is the chief of the spiritual beings who rebelled against God; sometimes he is called Lucifer, Prince of the Devils, and then there has also been the notion that there is a classification or category of angels or beings who have worked with Lucifer or who have assisted him. In a very recent statement by Pope Paul VI, he refers to the Chief of the Devils and to his assistants and cohorts.

Q: And those are the demons?

A: Yes.

Q: So it's a question of position really, not quality, more or less?

A: Yes, position.

Q: If the people in question, experienced the phenomenon they described, and I don't really have any reason to doubt them because others have experienced similar phenomenon in many cases, do you think that there is even the remotest possibility that somehow the divine system has made an exception for this one family in Amityville, Long Island, to send them a devil to do all these terrible things for reasons unknown, of course, or would you feel that this is simply a question of personal interpretation on their part?

A: I feel, personally, that it's a matter of personal interpretation. However, I think that it would be a mistake of rationalism to suppose that there *could* not be devils or to so imagine that anyone could know the divine plan to suppose that there could not be the possibility of this. It certainly is a possibility. But not a possibility that I would place much credence in.

7

Conclusions

As I look back upon the various interviews and investigations I undertook in and around the house and Ronald DeFeo, Jr, it appears to me that some factors about the spot emerged again and again, as separate from the house itself. It is also clear from my interview with the curator of the Amityville Historical Society, that the facts concerning the location are not as widely known as one would suspect them to be. For that reason I had early in the proceedings engaged the services of a professional researcher, Laura DiDio, who was then a production assistant at Channel 5 Metromedia television. Here is what Miss DiDio discovered after visiting Amityville in late 1976.

'The house was built in 1928 by a man named Monahan for his family. He left the house to his daughter and her husband; their name was Fitzgerald. The house then passed on to Mr and Mrs Riley. Several months ago I spoke to Mrs Riley whose name is now Malone. According to her, nothing out of the ordinary ever happened in the years that she and her husband owned the house. When I inquired why they sold it she replied that they got divorced. Shortly afterwards the house was purchased by the DeFeos. When they moved in they were apparently a happy family. Then something started to go wrong. Ronald DeFeo started on drugs and often fought with his family, he ran away from home on at least three occasions, but each time his family found him and brought him back. He pleaded with them not to do so because he said he knew he was going to kill them, which, of course, he later did.

'In conversations with family friends, relatives and neighbors it seems that the DeFeos were convinced that there were forces beyond their control in the house. Ronald DeFeo, Sr had a priest come in and say a Catholic mass in the house and I am told with all the windows shut, a wind came up and blew out the candles. DeFeo didn't stop with masses, he got statues of saints and placed them on the front lawn and bought tulip plants. All the plants died except for the one that was planted for DeFeo's daughter Allison. Allison, although friends report that she was afraid of her brother Ronald, seems to be the calm eye in the center of the storm. The Lutz's reported no disturbances in the room that had been hers when they moved into the house. It was also curious that at all times when I was present in the house with various psychics that they all had the same reaction upon entering the second-floor bedroom that had been Allison's – relief and a sense of peace.

'The house that now stands at 112 Ocean Avenue is not the original house that was on that piece of property. The original house was moved and now stands several blocks away on the corner of Carmen Street and South Island Place. Upon researching the history of the house I found that it stands on what was once an Indian burial ground. Back in the 1700's there was reportedly witchcraft practiced by some of the former owners. One of the psychics who visited the place got the impression of a Jamaican, a West Indian maid who was knowledgeable in voodoo, but I was never able to confirm this.'

From all indications it appears that Ronald DeFeo, Jr changed radically upon entering the house in question, although prior to moving there he had already exhibited certain violent tendencies. This, unfortunately, was used to make a case against him, whereas from the point of view of parapsychology it also indicates that he was a good subject for possession. For possession takes place when the subject is already inclined to emotional disturbances, and the possessor can then mold the personality with greater ease to his or her own whims. This, of course, would not be readily acceptable in a court of law. But nevertheless represents my firm conviction, and based upon this and other cases of possession, I am very sure that the voice within which told Ronald DeFeo to kill was not his own.

Other, marginal theories remain. There are those who think he didn't commit the crime, after all, and that someone else did it in his presence and framed Ronald DeFeo, Jr. He himself is not sure of what exactly happened, and yet he maintains he did not do it, that is to say, as Ronald DeFeo, Jr. Also, the figure with black hands handing him the gun is a fascinating item: was it his sister Dawn, as Ronald claims, or was it someone a lot less substantial appearing to him for the purpose of beginning the slaughter?

When I first entered the case it was my feeling that DeFeo had committed the physical crimes and could not be exonerated for them. At best, if the trial were reopened, mitigating circumstances could be brought out, such as possession, to lessen the severity of his penalty. Now, as I look back upon greater and more mysterious details of the case, I am not even sure of that. If he did indeed commit the physical crime, as it seems likely, but not completely definite, then of course he could not be held morally responsible for what was done with the vehicle of his physical body. If he was being used by forces beyond our physical world to do their bidding, then his own will was totally excluded from the action. In that case, incarceration for the rest of his life seemed out of proportion with the deed. In the final analysis, no one could punish Ronald DeFeo,

Jr any more than he already has done himself: having to live for the rest of his life with the knowledge that he had either willingly or unwillingly murdered six members of his own family, seems punishment enough.